Interference powder

BY JEAN HANFF KORELITZ

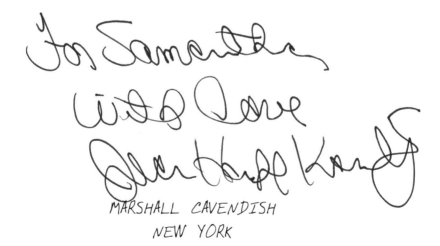

MARSHALL CAVENDISH
NEW YORK

FOR THREE OF MY FAVORITE GIRLS:
DOROTHY AOIFE KORELITZ MULDOON,
ELIZA ZOE NOVICK-SMITH,
GRACE ABIGAIL ECKSTROM ROSEN

AUTHOR'S NOTE

Interference Powder is real. It's made of ground-up mica, and artists use it by mixing it into paint or ink to lend a shimmer to their paintings and drawings. It does not have any magical properties. At least, I don't think it does.　　　　　—J.H.K.

Cavendish Children's Books
Marshall Cavendish
99 White Plains Road
Tarrytown, New York 10591-9001
www.marshallcavendish.com
Text copyright © 2003 by Jean Hanff Korelitz
Library of Congress Cataloging-in-Publication Data
Korelitz, Jean Hanff, 1961-
Interference powder / by Jean Hanff Korelitz.
p. cm.
Summary: Fifth-grader Nina Zabin happens upon a strange powder that causes events in her life to change, and not always for the better, as the school's Brain Buster Extravaganza approaches and she takes her best friend's place as representative for their class.
ISBN 0-7614-5139-0
[1. Magic—Fiction. 2. Schools--Fiction. 3. Contests--Fiction. 4. Drawing—Fiction. 5. Mothers and daughters—Fiction.] I. Title.
PZ7.K83646In 2003
[Fic]—dc21
2003000782
Book design by Pino Castellano
The text for this book is set in 12-point Souvenir ITC.
ISBN: 0-7614-5139-0
Printed in the United States of America
1 3 5 6 4 2

chapter ONE

What would you say if I told you there really was such a thing as a magic powder?

You'd say I was nuts, of course.

(Not that I'd blame you. I would have said I was nuts, too.)

And what would you say if I told you that this magic powder would make your wishes come totally true?

You'd say: "Well don't just stand there, hurry up and wish for a million dollars! Or a cure for cancer! Or a date with a movie star!"

But let me tell you, that is a bad idea.

In fact, it is one of the worst ideas in the universe.

Don't believe me?

You just give me a few minutes of your time. You'll believe me.

My name is Nina Zabin, and I'm going to spill it all. I'm going to tell you everything that happened to me after Interference Powder, and the way my mom met Dr. Serious, and how my aunt Sally found her passion, and also about Charlemagne and Isobel, and how I became an actual Brain-Buster, and why my toenails are probably going to stay purple for the rest of my life.

I know. I know. You're confused.

Well, I'm a little confused myself!

I'd better start out before the beginning, when none of these amazing things had had a chance to happen yet and I had never even heard of Interference Powder.

The morning of the day that Interference Powder happened was totally normal. I overslept five minutes, as usual, and my mom came clumping up the stairs and threw the covers off the bed. They landed in a big twist on the floor. She said, not really angry (not *yet*, anyway), "In five minutes there will be a hot piece of toast and a hot scrambled egg on the kitchen table. In six minutes there will be a cold piece of toast and a cold scrambled egg on the kitchen table. In seven minutes there will be NO TOAST AND NO EGG ON THE KITCHEN TABLE. So get up."

I got up. I had to. Without the covers it was freezing.

I got dressed and brushed my hair, which is long, brown, and straight, and put it up in a ponytail. I went into the bathroom and brushed my teeth. I rushed around looking for all the pieces of my homework, most of them not quite finished or sort of finished but messy, and one of them missing completely.

By the time I made it downstairs, my egg was almost cold. I plopped in my seat and started frantically looking for the history chapter I was supposed to have read the night before. My mom was sitting at the table, dressed for work but still in her bunny slippers. She was frowning at me over her coffee cup.

"A little behind, are we, Nina?" she asked.

"I forgot. We just finished up New Amsterdam. We were supposed to start on the Revolution. I mean, I did the reading, but we were supposed to answer these questions."

And so, that morning, over the cold egg and toast, the bunny slippers, and my open copy of *The Story of America*, my mother gave me The Look.

Let me explain about The Look. It's something my mom learned when she went to school to become a therapist after my father died. They teach you how to purse your lips, as if you're about to be forced to kiss somebody you don't like, and lift your eyebrows at the same time. That shows that you can see right through whatever story the patient is giving you.

"If you don't change your work habits," my mom said quietly, "you're going to be doing your homework at the breakfast table for the rest of your life."

I stopped and looked up at her. Homework? For the rest of my life?

"Oh, I don't mean math and social studies, Nina. But grown-ups have their own kinds of homework. We have to balance our checkbooks and pay our bills. We have to write letters and prepare presentations. What would happen if I raced into an appointment with a patient without having gone over my notes from past appointments? What if I hadn't made any notes? Or what if I made notes, but I stuck them in my pocket because I couldn't find the patient's file? And what if I had them in my pocket, and we went out to Burger King, and I left them on the table by accident? That would be terrible!"

"We never go to Burger King," I observed.

"No, but you know what I mean," she insisted. "Good work habits help you feel you're in charge of things. You know whether you've done what's expected of you, and there are no nasty surprises, like suddenly remembering you have an assignment and having to do it at the last minute." She drank her coffee, then looked at me squarely. "If you can figure this out now, Nina, you'll have more time for the things you really do want to do. That's the payoff."

That was the payoff, all right. I knew exactly what my mom was talking about. She was talking about singing lessons. I have only been wanting to take them for one hundred years, and I have explained to my mother many times that I will fall over and die if I don't take them soon; but she says I can't have them until I improve my grades. I've tried to explain that my brain isn't good at certain kinds of things, such as fractions and diagramming sentences. It's good at other kinds of things, such as music and making pictures. But my mom just doesn't understand. Looking at her stern expression, I knew better than to start our same old argument again.

Anyway, that's how the day of Interference Powder began.

chapter two

I left the house and walked to Riverside School, waiting at the corner of Wilton Street for my best friend, Isobel, to arrive. It was the first cool day of the fall. My last year's favorite black sweater was suddenly a little bit tight under the arms. I stood scowling as Isobel stopped short a few feet before the corner.

"What's with you?"

I held out my arms to show my naked wrists below the sleeves. "Too small. I love this sweater."

"Yeah," she agreed. "I thought you got bigger this year."

"I wish my clothes would get bigger with me," I sighed, shouldering my backpack.

"Well, when you grow up, you can invent that," said Isobel, stepping past me.

I laughed, but we both knew Isobel was far more likely to do something like that. She is the smartest girl in our class, but it's closer to say she's the smartest in our grade; and since we fifth graders are the oldest in our school, that totally makes her the smartest kid at Riverside.

Isobel lives on Robert Road in a house with a conversation pit and a fireplace hanging from the ceiling at one end. But what really makes her house special is the art, which is serious. Serious art! Isobel's parents are art professors.

When we were younger, I loved doing art projects at Isobel's house. Her mom and dad didn't just put out crayons or watercolor paint. Mrs. Grant had us doing mosaics with smashed china cups, or sculptures with fabric stained in tea or cranberry juice. But after a while her parents stopped trying. Although I was having a great time turning out pictures and collages, Isobel wasn't the least bit interested.

"You sure you're not our kid, Nina?" Mr. Grant asked me, gazing at a drawing I did of my house on Wilton Street, with its big maple and Fred, the dog from next door, asleep on the walkway in front. The fact is, I've always loved art, and I know I'm pretty good at it. Isobel, on the other hand, would much rather sneak out of the art studio to read in the girls' bathroom until the teacher figures out she's gone.

Anyway, on this particular morning I ran after Isobel on Prospect Street, and we walked the rest of the way to our school.

Our teacher, Ms. Tulane, is not the worst teacher we have ever had (that was Mrs. Manthis in second grade, who chewed her fingernails and then swallowed them), but she wasn't the best, either. She was at her desk, shuffling through a stack of papers, when Isobel and I came in. I knew what those papers were: our social studies tests from the week before. This had been the grand finale of the four weeks we'd spent on New Amsterdam—its society, history, and daily life!—a half-hour long groanfest of a test that included short questions and answers and a paragraph question at the end: "If you were a child living in New Amsterdam, what would your daily life be like?" I hated questions like that, and my mind had gone totally blank when I got to it, leaving me with only a little list of chores: tending the fire, milking the cow, baking the bread. These I had dutifully written down, hoping Ms. Tulane would ignore the fact that I hadn't come up with actual sentences, let alone a paragraph.

The test was important for another reason. Ms. Tulane had told us that the person who scored highest would represent our class against the other fifth grades at Riverside in the Brain-Busters Extravaganza, which had been dreamed up by our principal as a way of "fostering excitement about learning!" Basically, the extravaganza was like a spelling bee, with people having to answer history questions instead of spell words. The student who got the most answers right would be the winner. No one was enthusiastic about this idea, least of all me.

I already knew I'd got most of the answers on the test wrong. I'd never been best in the class on any test, and even if I did well, there was still Isobel. *Nobody* ever did better than Isobel; it was just unheard of. And for another thing, I had no desire to be the champion Brain-Buster of my class, let alone my school. The thought of getting up in front of a crowd and trying to say what my typical day was like as a girl in New Amsterdam gave me the jitters.

Ms. Tulane sat back in her chair and gave us a sour look. Out of the corner of my eye, I could see Isobel frowning to my right. She had figured out what those papers on the desk were, too.

"I wish I could say I'd had a pleasant weekend correcting your New Amsterdam tests," our teacher said, fixing us with a severe look. "But the truth is, I'm a little disappointed. It seems many of you have already forgotten the things we've been reading and discussing." She patted the stack of papers. "Of course, not everyone did badly, but overall I'd hoped for better results. Please bear that in mind as we move to our segment on the Revolutionary War." She sighed and got to her feet.

"I know you're all curious about who will be representing our class in the Brain-Busters Extravaganza," she continued. (In this she was much mistaken, I thought, since we all knew perfectly well who would be representing us—Isobel, of course.) "The highest score in the class was Isobel Grant's. A ninety-nine." She smiled brightly. "Congratulations, Isobel!"

"Thanks." Isobel shrugged, trying to hide her delight.

"I'm going to hand back your papers now," said Ms. Tulane as she moved down the aisle. "If you have questions, I'll be happy to answer them after class. You can take a moment or two to look over your papers, and then we'll open up our *Story of America* readers and start learning about the role Princeton played in the Revolution."

As she shuffled toward me, my heart sank. To my right, Isobel got her paper, and I caught sight of the big, red smiley face Ms. Tulane had written on the top, with a 99! beside it. Isobel smiled briefly, then shoved the paper under her *Story of America* book. I looked up and reached out my hand. Ms. Tulane frowned at me, then slipped the paper, blurry with red, into my palm. My heart sank.

A 62! Even I hadn't thought it would be that bad. Sixty-two was worse than great, worse than pretty good, even worse than just okay. Sixty-two was totally bad. I flipped through the pages. Red slashes cut through my short answers about the government of New Amsterdam, the price spent to purchase the island of Manhattan from the Native Americans, the social structure of the colony. And on the final page of the test, where the assignment had been to write an essay on what my daily life would have been like as a twelve year old in New Amsterdam, Ms. Tulane had written "Skimpy. I did not ask for a list, Nina."

Then, all at once, I realized that the test wasn't as unimportant as I'd told myself. Not, of course, because of the Brain-Busters Extravaganza, but because when my mom saw how badly I'd done, the subject of my much-longed-for singing lessons would be closed for good. If I couldn't get organized, if I couldn't manage to study, if I got a 62 on a test I'd had weeks to get ready for, there's no way I could convince her to let me add singing lessons and nightly practicing to my schedule. For a moment I thought I might cry, but I managed to freeze up my face in time. I didn't want anyone to think I was crying about the test itself. I didn't care about the test! I told myself. I didn't care about being as smart as Isobel. And I could care less about what my life as a girl in New Amsterdam might have been like! But I wanted to learn how to sing. And now it looked as if that would never happen.

I sighed, slipping the red-streaked paper into my math book, and opened my *Story of America*. I couldn't concentrate on the Battle of Princeton. By the time the class was over, I was as far behind on the American Revolution as I'd been on New Amsterdam. I got to my feet with a heavy heart. The fact that art class was next was only a small consolation. Even though I loved art almost as much as singing, I didn't think even that could raise my spirits today. Isobel, who did not love art, patted me on the back as our class left the room and made its way down to the studio.

chapter three

The art studio was at the end of the corridor. Its walls were splotched by years of flung paint, and pockmarked from thousands of thumbtacks. All sorts of stuff was pinned up, from kindergarten smudges to our own collage self-portraits, with papier-mâché objects dropping down from the ceilings to sway over our heads. One of my own paintings hung on the wall between two of the windows, and I smiled when I saw it. It was a picture I was kind of proud of: a study of Isobel's face, up close, her thin smile stretching across her face and her skin very white against a purple background. Isobel called this her vampiress portrait, which wasn't exactly a compliment. Still, I knew she liked the picture and felt proud to see it up on the wall.

When we got to the art room, I was surprised that Mrs. Smith, our teacher, was absent and in her place stood a tall woman with long hair in hundreds of little braids, some of them with beads and shells woven into their ends. The hair was mostly gray, but the woman's face wasn't really old. In fact, she looked around the same age as my mom. She grinned at us from the center of the room, with her hands thrust deep into the pockets of her big, faded apron, which she wore over jeans so worn they looked buttery-soft. In one ear she wore a long, dangly earring with a feather that brushed her shoulder. Nothing was in her other ear. Her fingers were bare, but her wrists clattered with little bracelets, silver and gold and every color. I stared at those bracelets. I had never seen anything like them.

Our class was bunched up at the door, uncertain about whether or not to enter, given that our art teacher wasn't there; but this different person motioned us inside, grinning all the while. "Come on!" she said gleefully. "Mrs. Smith is sick today, so I was called in. My name is Charlemagne."

Charlemagne! Isobel and I exchanged a look. Only the week before, Isobel's father had shown us a print of an old painting with a man in a chair. Four priests were standing over him, waving something that looked like palm fronds.

"Is he a saint?" Isobel had asked.

Her dad had laughed. "He thought he was. But no. He's King Charlemagne of France. Charles the Great! He made war on absolutely everybody."

And now, here we were, only a week later, confronted with one of Charles the Great's actual descendants, since what else could Ms. Charlemagne be? Imagine being descended from a medieval French king! How totally thrilling! Mom always told me that her great-great-great-uncle had invented the glue they use on the back of postage stamps, but that was nothing compared to being connected to ancient royalty.

Ms. Charlemagne began passing out paper as we drifted to the art tables. "I don't have any special plan today," she said. "I think we'll just see where our creativity takes us. Let's see what happens on the page. After all, that's what artists do, isn't it?"

Was it? I'd always thought they planned their paintings beforehand and then tried to make the picture on the canvas match the picture in their mind. That's what I always did, anyway.

The kids around me were picking through the pencil and crayon bins, looking at one another with uncertain expressions. They were used to being told by Mrs. Smith what the day's subject was or how they were supposed to make their pictures.

"Let's let the colors pick themselves!" Ms. Charlemagne chirped. "Let's let the pictures tell us what they should look like! Let's see what's on your mind today!"

I looked down at my blank white sheet. I knew what was on my mind. My low 62 grade, my never-to-be-had singing lessons, my mom's expression when she saw my test score tonight. I sighed and reached for a pencil. I began to draw my mother in our kitchen at home, her face pinched up in a frown. I drew her thin eyebrows and her eyes, with their pretty, curling eyelashes, looking down. I drew her hair falling forward a bit and one hand, the one that still wore my father's wedding ring, on the table before her. Next to that hand I drew my test; and just to make myself feel even worse, I drew my ugly score—62—right there on the paper. For a long moment I glared at it, as if willing it to change.

Then it struck me! I *could* change that number, at least here if not in real life. I could turn my pencil over and rub those terrible numbers away, then write new numbers in their place. I was the lord of my own picture, wasn't I? I could give myself a 63 on my social studies test, or a 61, or . . . why not even a perfect 100?

I tapped my pencil's eraser on the paper. It bounced a little under each tap, as if to say, "Come on! Come on already!" I bit my lip, considering. Then I rubbed at the 62. Three rubs and the numbers were gone, leaving a little dusting of pink rubber. I flicked that away with the side of my hand. In place of the 62, I wrote a perfect 100, just to see what it looked like.

A 100, on a piece of paper, next to my mother's hand, on our kitchen table, in my drawing. Now her frown seemed a little out of place. Why would she be looking so disappointed with a perfect 100? It looked wrong now, and I thought I'd better make it right, at least as far as the picture was concerned. I thought about it for another minute, then I rubbed away my mother's sour expression, erasing her mouth and then drawing it again, this time in a grin of delight and pride. Now my mother was happy, but I was feeling more depressed than ever. In fact, the picture made me so sad that I just stared at it. I didn't even hear Ms. Charlemagne come up behind me.

"Well, what a happy picture," she said softly. The music was still in her voice, but it was soft. "You draw so beautifully."

I felt really guilty, but I thanked her. I didn't think she would be so complimentary if she understood what I'd just done.

Ms. Charlemagne looked down. Her finger was tapping the paper.

"What about colors? What colors would this picture like to be?"

I bit my lip. "I don't know. I'm not really in a crayon kind of mood," I said; and to my surprise, she laughed brightly.

"I understand perfectly! This picture does not call for crayons, but it does need something." She seemed to consider the drawing. Then she said something strange. "You know," Ms. Charlemagne said. "I don't often get asked to substitute in an art class."

"Oh." I didn't know what else to say.

"No. Mostly I give lessons at home. But when I was called this morning, I thought I might just bring my old art kit with me, the one I used in college." She gestured with her hand, and I looked across the room to where she had hung her coat on a hook. Beneath it, on the floor, was a blackened and worn leather satchel, cracked with age. "There are lots of paints in there, though it's all a bit of a jumble, I'm afraid." She leaned closer to me, and her voice dropped to a whisper. "The truth is, it needs a good sorting out. It's been sitting around for years. Still, you might turn up something interesting if you'd like to look." She touched my shoulder lightly with one of her fingers. "You might find just the thing your picture needs."

Then she stood up and moved across the room to frown at Isobel's picture and gush at another girl's crayon drawing of a lipstick-red apple.

After a moment I got up too and crossed the room to Ms. Charlemagne's bag. It looked even older close-up, with dull brass buckles and a little brass button on the top.

I pressed the button, and the bag popped open with a click. Then I leaned over and peered inside. I couldn't make out much at first, just a bunch of old bottles in a jumble together, with bits of shredded rags and a few paintbrushes that looked really old. They didn't look like the plastic kind we use today. They could have been made of polished wood or bone. There was a strange smell coming from the depths of the bag, kind of old and mildewy, like a shower curtain that needs changing.

I reached inside with my right hand and lifted out a small glass vial. It was nearly empty, except for some dried-out blue grains at the bottom. It had a faded old label on which was written the word *cerulean*. That was a shade of blue, I knew. I picked up another, this one half full of packed orange grains, which read, in the same handwriting, Burnt Sienna. I knew that name from the back of a crayon box. I put the vial back inside and reached for a third. This one, to my surprise, had no color at all, just some loose flakes that weren't at all dried out and caked together like the others. In fact, when I gave the bottle a little shake, the flakes flew around in their little enclosure like those snow domes you shake to cause a flurry. And as they flew, something strange happened, but so fast that I thought I must have imagined it. The flakes changed to a sudden shimmer of color, and then, just as suddenly, that shimmer was gone and the flakes settled again at the bottom of the glass vial.

What color was this, anyway? I peered at the label, even more faded than the others, and it took me a full minute to decipher the handwriting. It read: Interference Powder.

Interference Powder? I frowned. What was *that* supposed to be? Was it a kind of medicine, like an old-fashioned sleeping remedy? Or something you planted in your garden to make the seeds grow better? But then why keep it in an artist's bag? I turned around to ask Ms. Charlemagne but found that Drea Wells was blocking my view. She was standing over me and looking down with a totally self-satisfied expression.

Drea Wells suffered from the well-known disease of I-am-better-than-you-itis. Anything a person could do, Drea Wells thought she could do better. Anything a person had to say, Drea Wells disagreed with it. Drea Wells had opinions on whatever a person might be wearing. She let no playground incident pass without inserting herself right into the middle of it. Her real name was Andrea, but that wasn't grand enough, so back in third grade she had gotten up in front of the class and announced that everybody had to call her Drea. If anybody called her Andrea, she would tell her mother, and her mother would call our mothers, and furthermore anybody who called her Andrea would not be invited to her eighth birthday party, which would really be a shame, since it was going to be a bowling party at Trenton Lanes with dinner afterward at King's Castle Chinese Restaurant. Then she had stuck her nose right up in the air and went and sat down.

I have no idea why Drea Wells turned out this way. When Isobel and I were four years old, we had had actual play dates with Drea Wells, and they were always fun. She had a very nice twin brother named Pip who was in Ms. Dravid's class and a very nice little sister in second grade who was always hugging everybody; but Drea seemed determined to make her way through life irritating everybody in sight. Isobel and I had especially detested her since fourth grade, when she told our teacher that Isobel was only pretending to read from *Little House on the Prairie* during independent study time like we were supposed to and actually had a different book open inside of it on her desk.

"Just what do you think you're doing, Nina Zabin?" she said, even though it was obvious she had already made up her little mind about what I was doing.

"It's none of your business," I replied, because it wasn't.

"Does our teacher know you're poking around in her personal things?"

I got to my feet, still holding the vial of mysterious powder. "Well, I imagine so," I said innocently, "since she told me to look for something in the bag."

"Then you won't mind if I tell her you've found something," Drea said, peering suspiciously at the vial.

"Not at all," I said, stepping past her. "You do that, Drea."

I walked back to my picture and sat down. Drat! I thought. Why hadn't I left the powder in the bag and taken one of the other colors instead? Whatever Interference Powder had been once upon a time, it was now just a ghost of its former self, a little pile of useless clear flakes. I looked up and met the squinty eyes of Drea Wells, who watched me from her seat across the room with an expression of keen interest. So I responded in the only way I could. I stuck out my tongue at her.

Then I twisted off the cap of the vial and shook a bit of the stuff over my drawing of Mom.

The flakes fell with a whoosh, hit the paper, and bounced up to make a little cloud over the page before settling again. As they did, it happened again—the sudden shimmer of color that had briefly filled the glass jar when I had shaken it: orange and blue, green and purple, bright red and pinpoint specks of black. All of the colors in the world, and then none of them. It happened so quickly that I could barely register the hues before they were gone. And then something else happened. As they hopped and settled, the lines of my drawing themselves began to hop: a little shudder of pencil marks, as if the floor beneath my chair had suffered one very tiny earthquake, so tiny that no one else in the room even noticed it had taken place—just me, and my chair, and my place at the art room table, and my picture lying flat before me sprinkled with clear flakes of Interference Powder. I blinked and shook my head.

I was startled by the arrival of Ms. Tulane in the doorway. The art class was over, and before I could signal the art teacher to ask her one of the two or three frantic questions zinging around in my brain, I saw Isobel moving toward my seat. I didn't want her to see the picture I had drawn. I didn't want her to know I had given myself that undeserved 100, even as a joke, so I quickly bent over the table and folded up the piece of paper, lengthwise first, then crossways, and shoved it into my jeans pocket. Then I raced across the room and put back the vial of flakes in Ms. Charlemagne's art bag. And that was how it all began.

chapter four

When school ended, I stood by my locker and waited for Isobel, the way I always did, so we could walk home together. But for some reason she didn't show up.

There was no explanation for this. Absolutely none.

I had just seen her in our homeroom, where we had both bent over our desks to write down the homework reading: two chapters on the Continental Army and an essay on some aspect of the life of George Washington besides the cherry tree episode. Then she was gone. After ten minutes or so I stopped waiting and walked home by myself.

I slipped inside my own front door, and I could hear my mom down in her office with a patient. The low, steady tones of her Voice of Concern came through the wall. I was still depressed because of Isobel not showing up and my rotten 62 on the New Amsterdam test, which was going to give my mom a total fit. I thought back through the school day: through history class and a boring game of Steal the Bacon in gym; through the lunchroom, where Isobel was strangely quiet and didn't seem interested in my description of Drea Wells's total obnoxiousness; back through math class, with its impossible fraction multiplications; back to my strange encounter with Ms. Charlemagne's decrepit artist's kit. Isobel, undoubtedly, was home by now. Already, I thought, she must have told her delighted parents about her 99 on the social studies test. Maybe that was it! Maybe she'd figured out about my 62 and that was why she'd avoided me after school, because she didn't want to rub it in.

But that was kind of strange. The truth was, I'd always been okay with Isobel doing better than me in school. In fact, I was planning to hold up a Go Isobel Go! poster at the Brain-Busters Extravaganza. I would even hurl confetti at her when she won. Surely she must know that by now.

But maybe not. Maybe I should call her and congratulate her, just to make her feel good.

I picked up the phone and pushed the buttons. She picked up on the second ring.

"It's I," I announced.

The "I" bit is one of our jokes. Mr. Grant, tired of hearing us say "It's me," had once given us a lecture about how "It's I" is grammatically correct. We've used it ever since.

"Oh," she said. Her voice was quiet and kind of tight. "Hello."

"Where were you after school?"

There was a pause. I was beginning to get a creeping, creepy feeling. Something was wrong. Something was most definitely wrong.

"Just home," Isobel said. Then she went silent again.

I remembered why I'd called.

"Is?" I said. "Listen, I forgot to say earlier, about that social studies test?"

"I have to go," she said sharply. "I'll . . . see you."

Then she hung up.

Isobel, my best friend, had hung up on me.

There had to be a mistake. I felt numb all over. There had to be something I didn't know. She couldn't be mad at me. Why would she be mad at me?

It had begun to rain heavily, and outside the sky grew very dark. I felt the warm fuzz ball that was our cat, Darwin, start to move about my legs as I stood there, still holding the phone.

Hang up the phone, you dummy, I told myself.

I hung up the phone.

Then I sat down at the kitchen table. I suddenly felt so tired. I had started to unload my backpack on the table when I came in; and I looked at the mess of books and papers now, thinking that the best way to get my mind off Isobel, not to mention that dumb social studies test, was to start my homework. But—and this is where I usually went wrong—the sight of my books just made me even more tired. I needed to go upstairs and rest before facing those horrible fractions again. I stumbled to the staircase and climbed to my room, diving for the pillow.

The next thing I remember was the smack of the fridge door being hurled shut (you had to hurl it or it would open up again) and the scrape of the kitchen chair: my mom.

I sat up. The clock read 6:00, which meant I'd slept longer than I'd intended. I stretched and rubbed my eyes. Then it hit me: my test! I hadn't planned to hide it from Mom, of course, but I'd been hoping to soften the blow as much as possible before she got a look at my terrible score. Now I bit my lip, trying to remember where I'd put the test in my backpack. Was it on top of my English notebook or wedged between my math and social studies assignments? Had I taken it out of my backpack already or was it still inside? Had my mom already seen it?

"Nina?" she called suddenly. "Nina! Come downstairs."

Angry?

Not angry?

It was impossible to tell.

I got to my feet, braced myself, and went downstairs.

She was sitting at the kitchen table with my books around her and one very particular piece of white paper right in front of her. Even before she looked up at me I felt strange—kind of woozy, as if the air had grown suddenly ripply with heat. I saw her face, my mother's face, and it was smiling. Smiling at me! I had this weird feeling in my stomach, like butterflies before you go onstage or get up to give a book report in class. My heart was pounding so loud, I almost felt as if I could hear it.

"Nina!" she said. "This is wonderful!"

What was wonderful? I looked wildly at her, and then my eyes fell to the page beneath her hands. It was my social studies test, but it wasn't, because this one did not say 62. It said, with great bold strokes of red ink: 100.

Oh no! I thought. I must have taken home Isobel's by mistake, and Isobel was even now reassuring her folks that the 62 in her yellow book bag was mine and not hers. But wait a minute—Isobel hadn't gotten a 100 on her test, either; she'd gotten a 99.

Who put that there? I thought, feeling so unsteady that I groped for the banister behind me. What kind of mean person would play this sort of trick, and why? Would my mom think I'd changed it myself? Could she really think I'd stoop so low as to change my own test score?

But wait a minute . . . that's exactly what I'd done, only hours earlier, on that drawing I'd made in art class. I'd rubbed out the 62 with my own hand and written in 100. But so what? What did my art class drawing have to do with the real, actual social studies test? It was totally impossible.

I reached out and took the test from my mom. The red 100 was surrounded by little smiley faces, the kind I had seen hours earlier on Isobel's test. I scanned the page of short answers, each and every one of them written in my handwriting, each checked off with a big, happy check mark. And on the last page, where Ms. Tulane had asked us to describe our typical day as a twelve year old in New Amsterdam, I was stunned to read—in rather nicely composed and fact-filled sentences—about the busy daily schedule of Nina Zabin, resident of New Amsterdam, circa 1650. It was mine, all right. Except for the small fact that I hadn't written it.

"Nina!" My mom was positively grinning. "Aren't you pleased?"

Pleased? I wanted to scream! It was all wrong. I wasn't responsible for that 100, and I certainly didn't earn it.

"Sure," I heard myself say. "But I didn't actually do that great on the test."

"Not great?" She laughed. "Since when is a 100 not that great?"

"No, I mean . . ." I trailed off. What *did* I mean? If I told her about my drawing, wouldn't she rush me straight to the hospital? And not only that. My mom seemed so happy and so proud of me. I couldn't stand to think of watching that smile leave her face. "I didn't really study that hard."

"Well, obviously you studied hard enough." My mom got up. She came around the table and hugged me across the shoulders.

I hugged her back. I couldn't help it; it was all so unusual, this pride in my schoolwork, and it was so . . . nice. Mom told me she'd made my favorite, spaghetti with olive oil and garlic, for dinner and shooed me off upstairs with my backpack and a friendly word about getting started on my homework.

I clomped up the stairs, my heart heavy. When I got back to my room, I sat hard on my bed, letting the backpack fall to my feet. Beneath me, something gave a funny crackle.

What was that? I frowned and felt underneath me. There, in my back pocket, was the folded-up picture from art class. The picture in which I had changed my own bad grade to a perfect grade I had not earned. The picture in which I had changed my mother's frown to a smile of delight—the same smile of delight I had just seen on her face downstairs. The picture that I had sprinkled with a mysterious and unknown substance called Interference Powder.

Interference Powder. And I had no idea what that was.

Thrilled and horrified, I pulled the picture from my pocket and raced to my desk, where I carefully unfolded it under a light. There was my smiling mother at the kitchen table, and there, my ill-gotten 100. In the creases of the page, Interference Powder still lay, dull and colorless, looking for all the world like the kind of crystallized sugar you sprinkle on top of a cupcake.

What had I done? And how would I ever undo it?

chapter five

The next morning, I had to wait longer than usual for Isobel on our corner. When she finally arrived, she moved past me without so much as a look.

"Hey!" I yelled, walking behind her. "Don't say good morning or anything."

"Okay," she said snottily. "I won't."

I paused, stung. Isobel had her moods, but she'd never had one lasting this long. I jogged up next to her. "Listen!" I said. "This incredible thing happened to me. It's so totally strange, I swear."

This did the trick. Curious, she looked at me as she motored along. "What happened?"

"My mom," I said, panting a bit. "She opened up my test from yesterday. It—listen to me, Is! It was the weirdest thing! When she looked at it, it had a 100 on it! A perfect 100!"

Isobel, far from stopping, only gave me a furious look. Never in all our years of friendship had she given me a look like that. It shut me up right away and hurt so much that I almost didn't hear what she said next.

"Why do you have to rub it in?" Isobel asked sharply.

Then she moved off, leaving me alone behind her.

Isobel? I thought dimly.

Rub *what* in?

It almost sounded as if she had already known about the 100 on my test; but that was ridiculous, unless . . .

I took a deep breath and gave words to the sick feeling in my stomach.

Unless . . . the Interference Powder had, well, *interfered.* Unless it had done something to me, to Isobel, to my mom, and to my test score.

But like I said, that wasn't possible. Once a thing had happened—like Isobel's 99, for example, or my 62, it couldn't *un*-happen, right?

I began to walk again. It felt weird to be walking alone, without Isobel. I had never, since starting kindergarten, walked into Riverside School without my best friend next to me, except on the days when Isobel happened to be sick. People might think it strange, our arriving separately like that. Would they know we had quarreled? And—wait a minute—*had* we quarreled? And if we had, what had we quarreled *about?*

In homeroom Isobel ignored me, and I sat at my desk with my face on fire, watching her all the time out of the corner of my eye. As if to make a bad situation worse, Isobel suddenly struck up a conversation with, of all people, Drea Wells. Their voices were low and their hands covered their mouths, as if they were afraid I might try to read their lips. But that was absurd—Isobel *despised* Drea, and always had. Or had that somehow been interfered with, too? I peered at them, feeling more miserable by the minute. What on earth could Drea Wells have to say that would be of the slightest interest to my best friend?

I thought I might cry, and I would have if Ms. Tulane hadn't arrived then and said something so horrendous that I promptly forgot about Isobel.

Our teacher went to her seat and looked at me straight away, then smiled. I smiled back, of course. I always smile at teachers, since I figure friendliness can only help make up for poor grades.

She hushed the room with one raised finger. "Quiet down," she said, looking in particular at the boys in the back row. They hushed beneath her steely gaze. "Now you'll recall, I hope, that our class representative for the Brain-Busters Extravaganza would be determined by our last social studies test. I want you all to join me now in a round of applause for Nina Zabin, who will carry our class banner, so to speak, when we go up against Ms. Dravid's and Mrs. Hampshire's class representatives next week." She looked around at them, a smile plastered on her face, and I was shocked to see that not a single one of my classmates looked surprised.

They knew. They all knew.

And what's more, they didn't look horrified about it.

They smiled at me and nodded, looking satisfied with their class representative. One or two gave me a thumbs-up, and even Drea Wells looked flushed with envy. But how was this possible? I was a student who scribbled my reports at the last minute, who guessed my way through long division, who tried—with mixed success—to make up in charm what my oral reports lacked in substance. I knew it, and my classmates knew it. So why did they look at me with such confidence? They couldn't actually believe I'd scored the highest in the class on that test, could they?

They could. And obviously they did.

I looked at Isobel now, though she was probably the last person to comfort me in these unusual circumstances, and sure enough, she was staring at her hands, which were folded on her desktop. Isobel! I thought, shrieking silently in her direction. But she wouldn't look at me. I hadn't really thought about it before, but now I saw that she had had her heart totally set on being our class Brain-Buster. Whatever I'd done, I'd done to her as much as to myself.

So I raised my hand. "Ms. Tulane?" I spoke quickly, afraid if I thought too long I wouldn't speak at all. "Can I, you know, step aside? I think I don't really want to."

Out of the corner of my eye, I saw Isobel perk up a little, but my teacher's smile faded. "Nina?" she said. "Come on up here. Class, you can start on your journals."

Everyone unzipped their backpacks. I made my way to the teacher's desk, and she leaned forward, speaking softly.

"Nina? What's this about?"

"I don't want to do it," I blurted. "I don't want to be a Brain-Buster. It was all a mistake."

She smiled and shook her head. "No mistake. Your test was the best in the class. You obviously knew the material extraordinarily well."

Extraordinarily well! I stared at her in horror. Not only had I not known some of the answers, but I'd forgotten just about *everything* I *had* known in the week since the test. The idea of getting up in front of the entire fifth grade with a head full of exactly nothing . . . Well, it made holding a tea party for a bunch of pythons sound relaxing by comparison. I leaned forward and whispered, "Please don't make me. Please, let Isobel. She'd be better at it."

Ms. Tulane considered. "I understand your difficulty, Nina. But we all need to learn new things as we grow up. You, for example, need to learn that you're not quite the so-so student you seem to think you are. And perhaps Isobel needs to learn that she won't always be the best at something.

It was all wrong, but I knew I could never make Ms. Tulane understand that. I had only wanted to make my mom happy! I never thought I would have to be a Brain-Buster.

I had started the day trying to work out how I'd explain to my mom what had happened, but now it looked as if I'd have to explain things to the entire world. And how was I supposed to do that if I myself didn't know?

chapter SIX

That evening my mom surprised me by saying she already knew about the Brain-Busters Extravaganza.

"Ms. Tulane called me at lunchtime," she explained, ladling minestrone soup into my bowl as I tossed some salad. "She told me how delighted she was with your grade on the social studies test."

"Oh," I said. I dumped some of the greens on my plate, making sure I avoided the red pepper. I didn't like red pepper.

"Ms. Tulane said you were going to represent the class in some kind of spelling bee or something. That's so great, Nina."

I shook my head. "Not a spelling bee. A Brain-Busters Extravaganza. And it isn't great; it's awful. I'm supposed to stand up in front of the entire school and answer questions about New Amsterdam. The whole idea is a rotten, nasty thing some evil genius of a principal dreamed up to torture the fifth grade. If you ask me, that person should have his own brain busted."

My mother sat watching me, a little smile hovering

around her mouth. "Now, this is interesting. Why can't you think of it as an honor to represent your class? Go to a couple of your classmates and ask them to help you study if you're worried. Make it a class project to get you ready."

A couple of your classmates, she said. Not Isobel. Did she know Is wasn't speaking to me? Had Ms. Tulane said something?

"Isobel's mad at me," I blurted. My voice sounded unnaturally loud, and I heard, beneath that loudness, the sound of my hurt. "She's mad she's not doing this dumb Brain-Buster thing. I wanted to change places with her, but the teacher wouldn't let me."

My mom tipped her soup bowl and lifted the last spoonful to her mouth. "Well, I'm glad about that," she told me. "You should be proud of your accomplishments, Nina. I'm sure Isobel did very well on the test, but this time you happened to do better. That's all."

I did lousy! I wanted to shout. But then I looked at her face, and there it was again: that look of pride.

"Besides," my mom went on, spearing a lettuce leaf, "I'm sure if Isobel told you she wanted to try her hand at something you've always been much better at, then you'd be really supportive and encourage her all you could. Am I right?"

I imagined Isobel becoming an incredibly talented artist or, better yet, even a singer. I imagined her walking onto a stage and stopping at a piano, her hand resting lightly on top of it and the people in the audience hushed, waiting for her to begin. I imagined them leaping to their feet when she had sung her last note, wildly applauding, and I imagined the critics writing about her totally amazing voice filling the dark room. There was an unmistakable pang as I thought of these things, yet even as my skin pricked with envy, I understood that I could never wish for bad things to happen to Isobel. I knew I would always help her and praise her efforts. She was my best friend, and I only wanted great things to happen to her.

And this was the same Isobel who hadn't spoken to me all day! When I'd hung around after school, hoping against hope that she would walk home with me, she brushed past and stomped off in the direction of our houses.

Thinking that made me want to cry.

And all this trouble because I'd sprinkled something called Interference Powder over a perfectly ordinary drawing.

I stopped in midchew. If it had happened once, couldn't it happen again?

"You okay?" my mom asked. She glanced at my plate. "Sorry, sweetie. I forgot about you and red pepper."

"No, it's okay," I said. "I mean, I'm fine."

"Still thinking about Isobel?"

I nodded, my thoughts racing. I wasn't thinking about Isobel. I was thinking about the Interference Powder, which was upstairs in my room.

Last night, when I'd unfolded my drawing and found the strange flakes trapped in its creases, I knew I shouldn't throw anything away. I'd carefully poured the powder into an envelope and stashed it in the top drawer of my bedside table. And as for the drawing— well, I'd kept that, too, of course. The whole thing had been pretty straightforward the first time around, hadn't it? Draw a perfect test score, get a perfect test score? Well, this time I would just give myself back the 62 I deserved and that would be that. Maybe the first time it had all been an accident, but if I did it again I'd be able to control it. After all, I was the artist—that meant I was the boss!

Quickly, I refilled my glass of apple cider from the fridge and started to concentrate on what my new picture should look like.

"Nina?" My mom raised her eyebrows. "We done talking?"

"What?" I frowned. "Oh. No, of course not."

"Want to hear about my day?"

I didn't, actually. I wanted to leave the table so I could get upstairs and fix my drawing, but I didn't want to hurt my mom's feelings.

"Sure." I smiled, gulping my cider, and she started to talk about the call she'd had that morning from Aunt Sally, and how Aunt Sally had decided she was tired of being a real estate lawyer and how she was going to go on a retreat for women where they helped you figure out what you were really supposed to be doing with your life.

"You mean, you go on this retreat, and some stranger looks at you and says, 'You should be a dog beautician' or something?"

"Well, I think there's more to it than that, Nina. I think they ask you lots of questions and help you figure out what your passion is."

"What your what?" I looked at her.

My mom set down her glass. "You know. Your passion. No"—she shook her head—"I don't mean moons and flowers, silly. It's not the same kind of passion as falling in love. It's your passion for work. It's doing work that makes you feel you're using the best part of yourself. Like when I help my patients, I feel I'm using the best part of myself."

"How do you help them just by talking to them?" I asked, because her work was really mysterious to me. I knew about the Look of Concern and the Voice of Concern, of course, but other than that, the details seemed kind of vague.

"Well, for example, if a person is very unhappy and doesn't see a way to get out of the unhappiness, I can sometimes guide him or her. Or if a person is having a hard time communicating with someone, then I can help them find a way to make a connection with that person."

This, as usual, was very vague. I'd been hoping for something a little more specific.

"Can't you be more specific?" I asked.

"Well, you know I can't," she said. "What happens

between my patients and me is private." She considered. "But here's something I can tell you. I once had a patient who possessed a wonderful talent, but it was a talent that required her to get up and perform in front of people. Unfortunately, she developed a terrible fear of performing publicly, so for many years she couldn't use her talent. Well," my mother said, "that's not entirely true. She used it to teach other people, but she couldn't really fulfill her own capabilities. She kept having to turn down offers to do what she loved to do, and it made her very sad. Then, a few months ago, after we'd been working together, she was invited to appear before an audience again and do what she was so good at."

"And?" I said.

"She did it. She was wonderful, and it made her very happy. So I helped her, and I used the best parts of myself to do it. I used my own intelligence and my own compassion, and I used what I've learned, both in school and from my own life and from my other patients. And that makes me feel wonderful. That's my passion for my work. Now if my job were something different, like working in a shop, for example, I don't know if I'd feel that way."

I thought for a moment, then looked up at her. "What's my passion?" I asked.

She smiled at me. "I wouldn't know. And you probably don't know, either. At least, not yet. One day you might drift into some kind of work that you love, and you'll want to spend your life doing it. Or you might get excited about some subject and want to devote yourself to studying it.

"You mean, like a college professor? Like the Grants?"

"Yup," she nodded, but I thought it was pretty unlikely that I was going to find my passion in school. If I was going to find it at all, I thought, it was probably going to be in an artist's studio, or a theater, or some place like that. Sometimes I wondered how my mom could know me as well as she did and love me as much as she did but at the same time understand so little about me.

"Aunt Sally always said she was going to go to law school," my mom continued, "but, to tell you the truth, she never talked that much about actually *being* a lawyer. I'm not surprised her work isn't making her happy. Practically *every* time I call her she's out in her backyard, making chairs."

"Chairs?" I stopped eating.

"Yeah. She made a chair to sit outside in her garden. She said all that sawing and hammering relaxed her so much that she started making chairs for all her friends." My mom paused and shook her head. "Anyway, I just want her to be happy. I mean, as happy as I am."

I thought of my mom on the phone with her sister, saying how lonely she was sometimes since my dad died. I knew Mom wasn't always happy.

"You mean, happy in your work."

She gave me an odd little look. "Yes. I mean in my work."

Then she got up to clear the dishes and started to talk about an article she had read in the local paper that morning, about the garbage cans in our town and how a group of citizens had decided they needed to be prettier, and so a committee had been formed to insist that something be done. "What a town!" She chuckled, putting her dish in the sink. "Too many people around here have a bit too much time on their hands."

I tried to look interested, but my thoughts wandered to Isobel, and the Brain-Busters Extravaganza, and what I was going to do as soon as I could get upstairs.

chapter seven

The Interference Powder was right where I'd left it, in a plain envelope in my bedside drawer. My picture was there too, folded neatly and weighted down by a geode Isobel gave me for my last birthday. I took the picture out and smoothed it, guiltily meeting the happy gaze of the mom on the page. "Sorry," I told her as I took an eraser and rubbed out the 1, then the first 0, then the second. All gone. My test was a totally blank slate.

Now, I won't say I wasn't tempted to give myself a 98! A 98 would have meant I'd still done fabulously well on my test, just not as fabulously well as Isobel, who thus would have been made our class Brain-Buster. But I thought I'd better not take any more chances of things going wrong. A 62 was what I'd earned, and a 62 was what I must have. I flicked away the last of the bits of eraser and wrote 62 clearly in the same spot.

And there it was. Now my mom looked a little *too* proud of me—after all, I'd only gotten a 62!—but just seeing that number on the page gave me a feeling of relief.

It was time for the powder. I tried to remember if I'd sprinkled it in any particular way, but nothing came to mind, so I just tipped open the envelope, and the little specks fell through the air onto the page.

I held my breath, watching.

Ten seconds passed.

There was nothing. No shimmer like the burst of colors I'd seen in the art room. No little vibration as the grains hit the paper and then jumped upward again. No pencil lines wriggling to life. Above all, no sense that something had *happened*, something unusual and unexpected. Something . . . well . . . magical.

It hadn't worked. And then, without even thinking too carefully about it, I understood why it hadn't worked.

The picture was old. It was used. And the Interference Powder knew it.

You couldn't go back and repeat magic, and you couldn't fix it; you could only go forward and make something new.

I would have to start again, with another picture. I would have to get what I wanted by approaching the problem in a completely different way.

Frowning, I got up and started to pace around the room. Darwin, eyeing me warily from the bed, got stiffly to his feet and walked to the door. He nudged it open and disappeared into the hall.

I tried to imagine that I was back in the art room at my school. I wanted to do everything just the same way

I had done it before. First of all, the same paper . . . yes, I had plain white paper. I went and got some and brought it to my desk in front of the window. The same pencil. Well, I didn't have the exact same pencil, but I had a plain one like the one I'd used in Ms. Charlemagne's class. I got that, too. I sat down. What else? Did it matter what I had been wearing yesterday? Or the way my hair had been pulled back? Did it matter how I'd been sitting at my desk? Or that there'd been a Band-Aid on my right heel, because a pair of new shoes I'd worn over the weekend had left me with a blister, but now the blister was healed and the Band-Aid gone?

My head started to spin. I couldn't possibly get everything the same. I understood that. But the important stuff—the paper and pencil, and the way I'd sprinkled Interference Powder like salt from a shaker—I could do that again. I closed my eyes for a minute in concentration and thought about my picture. Then I started to draw.

This time I wasn't drawing my mother, or my test, or even myself. This time I drew Isobel. I drew her wearing her favorite pink sweater and blue jeans and the green string of love beads she had made at the bead shop on Witherspoon Street. I drew her grinning, her mouth open in midspeech. I drew the auditorium, with the Riverside School banner behind her and the other banner reading First Annual Brain-Busters Extravaganza! floating above her head. I drew round humps—the heads of kids—in front of her as an audience. For a moment I considered putting myself into the picture too, off to one side perhaps and cheering Isobel on, but something told me to keep it simple. After all, the more stuff I put into the picture, the more things that could go wrong.

When the picture was done, I brushed it with the back of my hand, flicking away dust and flakes of pencil lead, then blew the page to get it totally clean: a blank slate for the magic, or whatever Interference Powder actually was. Then I set down the piece of paper. I couldn't think of anything else I needed to do.

Biting my lip, I picked up the first drawing of my mom and folded it so all the grains slid to the center of the paper. Then I closed my eyes and shook those crystals over my new picture. Work, I thought, concentrating hard. Please work. Please put Isobel on that stage instead of me. She belongs there. She's the truly smart one who doesn't need Interference Powder to do well on a social studies test. And please make us friends again. I had only had one day without Isobel, and already I missed her so much I couldn't stand it.

And that's when it came: that little ripple I remembered, that strange quickening in the air. I opened my eyes in surprise, just in time to see the end of the color dancing in the air. But I couldn't be sure, because this time there were tears in my eyes making my vision blurry, and suddenly I heard a little splat as one of those tears hit the paper. I stared down at it in horror.

Interference powder

My tear lay on the stage in my drawing, looking like a little puddle plopped down in the middle of the floor; and right in the center of it, floating on the surface, there was the unmistakable shimmer of Interference Powder.

chapter eight

The next morning, when Isobel once again brushed past me and kept right on walking to school, I knew that something had gone wrong. I wasn't sure what, but Isobel was acting the same unfriendly way she had acted yesterday. With a sinking heart, I shouldered my backpack and trudged on to school.

In my classroom, Ms. Tulane had hung my photograph behind her desk, with the words Our Class Brain-Buster! written above it. Gritting my teeth, I thought about writing to the school board and telling them what a totally bad idea this whole thing was and that our principal, Mr. Arthur, who thought up the Brain-Busters Extravaganza, had no idea what fifth graders are like. No one in fifth grade liked to risk being humiliated in front of a group. He must have skipped fifth grade altogether, or perhaps even his entire childhood. But how could I write a letter like that without raising all sorts of questions about myself and about the social studies test that had made me my class Brain-Buster?

I sighed. Behind me, Drea Wells was snorting something at Isobel. I turned and saw Isobel shake her head—not laughing in agreement, but not ignoring her, either. I looked hard at Isobel. Then I tried to smile when I caught her eye, and for a moment I thought she was about to smile back; but just as she seemed to be making up her mind about that, our teacher came in.

"Sorry to be late," said Ms. Tulane with a cheery lift to her voice. "But I've just come from a little teachers' meeting. I think you'll all find this interesting."

Everyone waited. To my left, Henry McKenna leaned forward, looking worried. The last time there had been a teachers' meeting, it had been about Fortune Soldier Action Heroes, which were taking over the entire school, from kindergarten on up. The meeting, which was called to decide how to handle fifty boys Action Hero-fighting during recess, had come up with the rule to ban all Fortune Soldier Action Hero figurines, games, playacting, and pretend fighting on school premises. This was a rule particularly unbearable to Henry McKenna, who had collected more than twenty-five of the foul little creatures. I could tell he was wondering what unfair rule was about to be announced this time. But it had nothing at all to do with Henry, as it turned out. It had to do with Isobel, of course, and with me, of course, of course. And I was about to find out what that Something Awful was.

"We've been thinking," Ms. Tulane began, taking her seat, "about ways to make the Brain-Busters Extravaganza more of a class project. That is, something you can all participate in, not just the three students representing each of the fifth-grade classes. So we've decided that we teachers should not be asking the questions at the extravaganza but that representatives from each class will actually write and pose the questions." She smiled brightly at me, as if this change of events was supposed to make me happy.

"The way it's going to work is that all of you . . . except Nina, of course"—she chuckled—"all of you will get together and come up with the questions for the three class representatives. Naturally, you will not discuss your questions with any of those three students! Then those questions will go into a box with the questions each of the other two classes have provided. And the questions we choose on the big day will come out of that box."

Hands shot up. Were the questions in the box supposed to be easy or hard?

A mixture, Ms. Tulane said. After all, some of our class's questions might go to our own class representative. An overly difficult question would be hard for us if we got that question, but an overly simple one would be bad for us if another class representative got it.

Could they pick which contestants got which questions? (This came from Drea Wells, naturally.)

No, said Ms. Tulane. The whole point was that they would be picked out of the box.

Who would get to ask the questions, asked Isobel, and here Ms. Tulane smiled.

"Well, as a matter of fact," she said, "we've decided

that the student who scored second highest on our social studies test would have the honor of picking out the questions and asking them at the extravaganza. That's you, Isobel."

And then Isobel sat up straight and turned to look right at me. She didn't smile. She didn't gloat. But her eyes said, as clear as if she'd yelled out the words: *Now you'll get it.*

And I got it, all right. My drawing, with Isobel onstage, grinning and happy, the Brain-Busters Extravaganza banner hung behind her. Exactly as I'd drawn it but, of course, far from the way I'd planned. Interference Powder had struck again.

chapter nine

After that the morning got worse. First came a math class so boring, I thought I might fall over in the aisle; then at lunch Drea Wells sat in the seat I always sat in, next to Isobel. I had to sit with Henry McKenna and a few of his like-minded morons. One of them asked me if he would get to bust my brain if I blew it at the extravaganza. He laughed so hard when he said this that he actually sputtered a few drops of apple juice across the table in my direction. They fell on my plate next to my grilled cheese sandwich.

In the afternoon, Ms. Tulane sent me to the library while the rest of my class drew their chairs into a circle to begin thinking up questions about life in New Amsterdam. When I entered the green-carpeted room lined with books, I spied my two fellow victims: Theo Matza, who was representing Ms. Dravid's class, and a girl from Mrs. Hampshire's class I knew only as Ella since she was new in our school. They were sitting at separate tables and already hard at work, their noses buried in *New Amsterdam Days and Ways*. I said a tiny little hello, took a seat at another table, and started going through my old social studies notes. Then I opened my book and started to read.

I read about the first families to arrive in New York Harbor and their agreement with the Dutch West Indies Company that was sponsoring their journey to the New World. I read about their purchase of the island of Manhattan for a lousy twenty-four dollars in beads and doodads from the unfortunate Algonquin Indians. I read about their farms and their forts and their governors and one-legged Peter Stuyvesant himself. I read about their sheep, goats, pigs, cows, chickens, ducks, wild turkeys, and partridges, and about the wild foxes, possums, wolves, and bears that also roamed the island. I went back over all the stuff I would have had to do around the house if I'd been a girl in New Amsterdam: spinning and sewing and cooking in the fireplace, churning butter and making candles and growing herbs in the garden and making birch brooms. And I read again about the house I would have lived in, with its roof steps to reach the chimney and its red tile roof, a Dutch door (good for keeping out the animals while chatting with the neighbors), and a front stoop.

At the other tables, Ella and Theo shifted in their seats and turned their pages. I glanced at their faces to see if they resented this as much as I did, but they looked happy enough to be in the comfortable library chairs, reading their books while the rest of their classes huddled and schemed together.

Ella had a single thick black braid, neat and tight

down the middle of her back except for a little piece of hair that had worked totally loose behind one ear. She twisted this piece around one finger as she read, only occasionally leaving it alone to turn the next page of her book. Ella wasn't just new at our school, she was new in our town. I was pretty sure she came from California, since most of her T-shirts had the word California on them somewhere: California State U., California Beach Academy—Study the Surf!, Certified California Girl. Isobel and I had had a good giggle about that, I remembered. I had talked to her exactly once in my life, in the cafeteria, and that was to steer her away from the Swedish meatballs.

Theo and I, on the other hand, had been in kindergarten together, and since then we'd been in the same class more than once. I'd always sort of liked him, not only because he was friendly but because I had never once seen him with a Fortune Soldier Action Hero.

"Theo," I whispered, leaning forward in my seat.

He looked up from his book. "Hmm?"

"Listen. Don't you think this is kind of dumb?"

Theo frowned. "What? You mean the Brain-Buster thing?"

I nodded. "I think it stinks. I don't want to do it."

He sighed. "I know what you mean. I had a long talk with my dad about it, and he agrees. I mean, he's proud of me and all, but I have no desire to wear a hat that says Smartest Kid in the Class. I don't know what your class is like, but I had a hard enough time before it became official."

I looked at him in surprise. He was, as always, very humble about his superior intellect. I didn't think he should get teased about it.

"Has someone been obnoxious to you?"

He looked sadly down at his book. "Nothing I'm not used to. But it's kind of a no-win situation for me. If I lose this stupid thing, everybody will be mad at me. But if I win I'm not going to suddenly turn into Mr. Popular."

I glanced over at Ella. She had put down her book and was listening.

"Let's protest!" I said. "Let's go to the principal and say none of us wants to do it. We'll say it's a dumb idea to make learning into a competition."

"But they'll think we're scared," Ella said.

And they'll be totally right, I thought.

"Besides," said Theo, "if we don't do it, they'll only pick someone *else*."

"Then they'd *really* say we were scared," Ella said.

"So we're going to be shamed into doing something we don't want to do?" I said, sounding angry. "We should make a pact not to answer questions!"

"A strike." Ella smiled. "I had an uncle who went on strike at the restaurant where he worked. After a week the owner gave all the waiters a raise."

"You know," Theo said brightly, "it's just like this movie I saw, about this gladiator in Rome who doesn't want to fight. They keep putting him in the ring with another gladiator, and he refuses to lift his sword."

"So what happens to him?" I asked.

Theo wrinkled his forehead. "Can't remember."

Ella looked at me and shook her head. "Why don't we just agree to have fun and not take it too seriously? It's not like an IQ test or an SAT or anything like that. What's the big deal?"

Theo considered, then nodded at us both. "We could have a study party, the three of us, and get ready for the dumb thing together. I mean . . . " He looked at us both, suddenly shy. "If you wanted. You could come to my house for dinner the night before. We could quiz each other."

Ella looked at me. "Sure."

"Okay," I told him. I kind of liked the idea. Dinner at Theo's house? Studying with Ella, whom I'd barely gotten to know?

And so, with embarrassed shrugs all around, the two of them opened their books and went back to studying. I did, too. After all, what choice did I have?

chapter ten

I know what you're thinking. You're thinking, What an idiot Nina is! If she had half a brain, she'd track down that art teacher with all the little braids and get her to explain how to make Interference Powder return things to normal!

Well, I do have half a brain, thank you very much, and that's one of the first things I tried.

Charlemagne. You'd think there wouldn't be too many people with that name in Princeton, and you'd be right. In fact, there weren't any. I tried the surrounding towns: Hopewell, West Windsor, Montgomery, Lawrenceville, Trenton. No Charlemagnes. I even went to the public library and used a computer to search for Charlemagnes, and there was one—in South Dakota. First name, Herbert.

I thought hard, trying to remember every little thing I could about Ms. Charlemagne. Hadn't she said she didn't often substitute because she usually gave lessons at home? I raced for the Yellow Pages and looked up art schools in our part of New Jersey, then called to see if they had any Charlemagnes; but it was another dead end. After one final burst of inspiration, I went to the school office and asked if I could have the substitute teacher's number, because I wanted to find out about art lessons, but they wouldn't give it to me. I must have looked as if I was about to cry, because the secretary said she'd be happy to forward a letter if I cared to write one. Boy, did I care to write one! But even though I dropped my letter off the next morning, I didn't hear a thing in response.

I couldn't think of anything else to do.

A few nights later, on Wednesday, my mom drove me over to Theo's house on Cedar Street. I was balancing a platter of her roasted parsnips, covered with Saran Wrap, on my lap. After a series of telephone calls between my mom and Theo's mom and then Theo's mom and Ella's dad, our simple study dinner for the night before the Brain-Busters Extravaganza had mushroomed into a big parents' potluck. I'd noticed adults often did this sort of thing—took a simple plan like let's-get-together-and-study and changed it into a complicated arrangement involving food and extra chairs.

I knew what was in it for them. The opportunity to congratulate one another (wrongly, in my case) about how clever their children were—that's what they were after. And again, the thought of my mother's misplaced pride hit me with a fresh stab of discomfort. I shifted a bit in my seat, and some juice from the platter leaked onto my lap.

"Careful," my mom said, turning the corner.

"Got it," I reassured her.

"My famous MWRV." She smiled. "Right?"

I smiled, too. When I was younger, my mom once cooked a dish out of a really fancy cookbook written by a chef who had a television show. The dish was called Mélange of Winter Root Vegetables, and it required a ton of peeling. Only after my mom had cooked those vegetables and put them on the table did we recognize them for what they were: plain old boiled vegetables. So after that, whenever my mom made anything with a parsnip or a turnip or a rutabaga, we thought of the Mélange of Winter Root Vegetables, or MWRV, and laughed.

Ella and her father were getting out of their car when we arrived. Ella was carrying her copy of *New Amsterdam Days and Ways*. She looked at me and waved.

"This is my father," she called when my mom and I got out.

"Hi. Brian Serious," he said, and I almost laughed out loud. Poor Ella! How was she supposed to go through life with a last name like Serious? Seriously!

"Hello," my mom said, extending her hand. Ella's father was kind of on the big side, but most of his bulk came from the fact that he was pretty tall and had a way of hunching forward. Also, he wore a brown sweater so big that it sagged almost to his knees. He had curly black hair that looked just like Ella's, except it wasn't in a braid. "That looks good," said my mom.

"Tabbouleh." He grinned.

I made a face. I hated that stuff.

"Mmm," my mother said, and I gave her a look. She was being totally polite, I supposed, since she didn't like it, either.

As Ella and I climbed the front steps of Theo's house, she said, "I made some index cards today. I thought we could use them to quiz each other."

I looked at her. "That's a really good idea. I should have thought of that."

"I made some easy and some hard. Of course, I know the answers to them, but maybe you guys can come up with some questions for me."

"I'll try," I said. Index cards were a pretty good way to study for anything, especially if one could come up with the questions instead of trying to memorize the answers.

Theo opened the door for us, and his mom came rushing up behind him. "Nina!" she said happily, and I smiled politely, even though I wondered why she seemed so pleased to see me. "And Serena. Wasn't this a good idea?"

"It was Theo's idea," I said.

Mrs. Matza beamed at her son, as if this confirmed his superiority to all other boys.

"My mom brought parsnips," I said.

"Parsnips!" Ella's father came up behind my mother and looked over her shoulder. "I adore parsnips."

My mom totally blushed. "Oh. Well, I'm glad."

"C'mon, Nina." Theo was gesturing me inside. "Let's go in the living room. We can get in some studying before dinner."

"Great!" I said, though I wished we could go right to the food instead. My mother and Ella's dad were ushered into the kitchen, where I saw Mr. Matza standing over the stove. He was wearing a white apron and stirring something slowly and intently. As I watched, he put his hand into a bowl of something—Salt? I wondered—and sprinkled it over the contents of the pot. The gesture reminded me of Interference Powder, and I hoped whatever spell he was casting on our dinner did not misfire and turn his stew or casserole into chocolate pudding or Chicken à La Banana. I sighed and followed Ella into Theo's living room, where Theo placed a little bowl of pretzels beside each chair and asked if we would like something to drink.

Ella asked for a ginger ale. "I don't get to drink it at home," she confided.

"No?" I popped a pretzel into my mouth.

"My dad says soft drinks are a waste of calories. He says, if something has no nutritional benefit at all, you're better off not putting it in your body."

"Life without ginger ale." Theo shook his head. "That's very harsh."

But very fitting, I thought, for somebody named Serious.

"No fast food, either," she said.

"Well," Theo said, "my mom's not a big fan of fast food herself."

"Mine, neither. I never ate at McDonald's in my life till I was seven. Then I went to a birthday party there."

I stopped. The party had been Isobel's, and she'd only gotten her parents to agree to it after a six-month campaign of pleading. Remembering it now, and thinking of Isobel, made me sad again.

"I made flash card questions," Ella was telling Theo, and he thought this was extremely clever, so we popped the tops of our ginger ales and spread out the white cards on the table. Then, munching away at the pretzels, we began to pick them up and ask questions, though when it was time to ask Ella a question, Theo and I had to think up one. To my surprise, I started to relax after the first three or four had come my way, because even though Theo or Ella sometimes had something to add to my answer, I found that I knew more than I thought. Either Ella's questions were real softballs or I was fairly well informed on the subject of early Dutch colonial settlement on the island of Manhattan: Peter Stuyvesant's management style, a typical breakfast, the rights and responsibilities of settlers to the Dutch West Indies Company, religious practices, leisure time, crafts, laws, and law enforcement. After a while it got kind of interesting. We'd start talking about a topic of mutual interest to the three of us, except when we broke down in laughter because Ella began to answer her questions in a high-pitched Dutch girl voice. Then Theo said we should turn up the next day wearing wooden shoes or one of those silly hats they wore. I said none of us should go to school at all—we should all send a note from our doctors saying our brains had busted from studying so hard—and then Ella laughed and her ginger ale spurted down her chin and I went into the kitchen to get a paper towel.

There was no sign of Mr. or Mrs. Matza, but my mom was sitting at the kitchen table with Ella's dad, each of them holding a glass of white wine. "Oh," he was saying, "the banana house! I know the banana house! On Wilton Street, am I right?"

And she blushed. Again, like she had when Mr. Serious had complimented her parsnips. Then she noticed me.

"Oh. Hi, Nina."

"Hi." I frowned.

"Did you know Ella and her dad just moved here from Los Angeles?" She winked at me. "By which I mean . . . Hollywood."

"Hollywood!" I looked at him in surprise. "Why on earth would you move here if you lived there?"

My mother, quick as a wink, flashed me The Look.

But Ella's dad was smiling. He thought I was funny. "We forsook Hollywood for New Jersey, Ella and I, because Ella's mother decided to go to medical school. It's hard to get into medical school, but she got into one here, at Rutgers. So here we are."

"But . . . ," I said, "I thought . . . I mean, you're not married, right?"

"Nina!" My mother spoke sharply. "That's very personal."

I was surprised to see him briefly touch my mother's wrist. "No, it's all right. I realize that must be confusing. Yes," he said to me, "we are divorced, and yes, Ella lives with me and I take care of her most of the time; but she and her mom have a really important relationship, too. Important enough for us to move here, so we could all still be near one another."

Why not just stay married then? I thought, but for once I didn't say it out loud. Instead I chirped, "Well, that's nice," and went for the paper towels, which had been lurking in plain sight on the countertop the whole time. Then I went back to the living room and tried not to think about my mother and Ella's father, their heads almost touching over the kitchen table, their voices just low enough that I couldn't hear what they were saying.

chapter eleven

A little later, our parents brought us dinner on trays in the living room so we wouldn't have to interrupt our studying, and except for the tabbouleh, which I didn't eat, it all tasted wonderful: my mom's sweet parsnips, the smoky lamb stew from the oven in the Matzas' kitchen, the salad Theo and his mom had made earlier. The grown-ups ate in the living room, and we could hear them murmuring and laughing. After a while someone put on some jazz music, and even though it was low, I found it hard to concentrate. Luckily, Ella was having the same problem, so Theo invited us upstairs to his room. We had gone through all of Ella's flash cards by then, and we started getting sillier and sillier and thinking up really ridiculous questions, such as "Did they have Fortune Soldier Action Heroes in New Amsterdam?" and "If you were a kid in New Amsterdam, would you prefer rock 'n' roll or rap music?" Theo grinned when I suggested that Peter Stuyvesant stepped in a rabbit hole and lost his leg when the rabbit bit it off. Ella laughed so hard, she sputtered her ginger ale all over the place.

Theo's room wasn't like your typical boy's room. There were no sports posters, no rock group photographs, no computer games. Instead there were books—mostly from the town library—and a special kind of telephone for Theo to use when he talked to his older brother, Justin, who was away at college. Justin was deaf, and you had to type your message into the phone like a typewriter. And tacked to a big corkboard over the bed were pictures of Theo and his parents and Justin and a girl who looked shy and had super-straight black hair to her chin. Her name, Theo said, was Irina, and she was a pen pal who lived in Russia. "She wants to be a doctor," he explained. "She says her town really needs doctors, so she has to study hard because it's really difficult to get into medical school."

I nodded. Mr. Serious had just told me the same thing about Mrs. Serious, after all.

There was a school photograph next to Irina's picture, but it wasn't of Ms. Dravid's fifth-grade class; it was of our third-grade class, two years ago. I say "our" because third grade was the last time Theo and I were in the same class together. I stared at Isobel and me sitting cross-legged on the floor (next to each other, of course) and Theo standing and smiling in the second row between the Dorgan twins, Tara and Avery, who moved away from Princeton later that year. Behind him was Henry McKenna. Henry was holding up his fingers in a V behind Theo's head.

"What a jerk," I said out loud.

Theo just shrugged. "Sure, but jerks are everywhere. A person just has to learn to coexist peacefully with them."

"But why did you put this picture up instead of your fifth-grade one?"

"I don't know," he said. "I liked that class. I liked Ms. Bennet. I liked the kids. Not all the kids, but most of the group. I liked Isobel. I liked you."

And then I suddenly had this surprising thought. I thought: Theo is cute. Honestly. *Theo is cute!* Which I had never really noticed before.

"Isobel's mad at me," I said. I wasn't planning on saying it; it just slipped out.

Ella looked up. She frowned. I didn't think she knew who Isobel was, being new.

"Why's she mad?" Theo asked. "Because of this?"

"Well, sort of."

He shook his head. "Isobel. Remember in first grade when I beat her at Concentration?" He turned to Ella. "We had this whole competition going on in the playground. It went on for weeks. I won a game, then she won a game, then I won a game. It went on like that forever. People spent their whole recess under the big tree, you know, the one by the climbing ropes? Just watching us turn those cards over, looking for the pairs. So then finally, finally! I got two games up on her and she stormed off. I thought we'd keep on playing. I was having a good time! But Isobel . . ." He sighed. "She doesn't like to lose." Theo turned to me. "You remember."

"Yes," I said, because I did. I hadn't thought about it in years, but I did remember. She totally stopped playing Concentration after that. With me, too.

And then I remembered something else, something from way back, the first year Isobel and I were friends. We were at Thomas Sweet one afternoon with her mom, getting milk shakes, when we saw a sign posted by the door. Thomas Sweet was running a poster contest for kids. The poster had to say We Make People Happy! and have something to do with ice cream. Both of us entered. We filled out entry forms and went home and drew our posters at the Grants', using their art supplies at the kitchen table. Isobel drew an ice-cream cone with four scoops on it, and each scoop spelled out a word with chocolate chips: WE MAKE PEOPLE HAPPY. It was pretty, and she spent more time on it than she usually spent on her artwork; but her picture didn't win.

Mine won.

Mine showed a horse eating ice cream. Why a horse? Because I knew how to draw horses, that's the only reason. Cats? No. Dogs? No. But horses? For some weird reason horses were something I could draw. This horse was wearing a silly purple hat and eating a big bowl of ice cream and thinking (I made a thought bubble over her head, like a bumpy white cloud): "I don't know about people but . . . I'm happy!"

So I got my picture in the *Town Topics* newspaper holding a big ice-cream cone next to a picture of my poster. I won a punch card with ten ice-cream cones on it, which meant I got to have ten free ice cream cones at Thomas Sweet. But whenever I asked Isobel if she wanted to walk down Nassau Street for a cone, she said no, even though she loved ice cream as much as I did. I ended up eating all those free cones myself.

Theo was right. Isobel did not like to lose.

"Hey, I've got an idea," Ella said, interrupting my thoughts. "Let's each try to think up the three meanest, nastiest, hardest questions we can imagine, you know, the ones we don't want to get asked ourselves, and try them out on each other."

I nodded, and Theo said it was a good idea. We gave each other our meanest, nastiest, hardest questions, and, of course, we all answered them. And then, because there was nothing else we could do to get ready, we went downstairs.

My mom and I left Theo's house with smiles and waves and thank-yous for such a nice evening; and the funny thing was, I wasn't faking it at all. There had been a happy feeling between Theo and Ella and me, which is sort of funny if you think that the three of us were supposed to be in a fight-to-the-death competition the next morning! I remember shaking hands all around when we left to go home, and how nobody said anything annoying, such as, "May the best person win!"

You might think that finally things were beginning to look up. Wrong! The truth is, that's when I made what would turn out to be my biggest mistake of all.

chapter twelve

Later that night, I lay in bed. The house was dark and quiet, and the whole street was still except for Fred, the dog next door, who was prowling around the backyard. I couldn't sleep. I was thinking about the next day. My thoughts were going something like this:

I know I'm not going to win that stupid Brain-Busters Extravaganza! Oh, I might answer a few questions correctly; but eventually I'll come up against one that will stump me, and there I'll be, with my mouth opening and shutting like a fish, up on the stage in front of every kid I've ever gone to school with, and their little brothers and little sisters, and all my teachers, past and present, feeling like a complete idiot.

That's what would happen.

But—okay, let's pretend there's a miracle—let's say I win. I'd still come out a loser! Because then there'd be no hope that Isobel and I could be friends again.

I felt so hopeless, as if there was nothing at all to look forward to! Not the Brain-Busters Extravaganza, not Isobel, not singing lessons . . .

Hey, I thought. Wait a minute.

Maybe it was true that I couldn't fix the situation I was in. Maybe I was going to lose the stupid contest or maybe I was going to win it and lose my best friend. But shouldn't I get *something* for myself out of this mess? Some little thing I'd appreciate when it was all over? Didn't Interference Powder owe me that much?

This thought began to run around in my mind over and over again, as I listened to Fred in the backyard.

And then it came to me. Singing lessons!

I sat up in bed. I said to myself, "Nina, don't even think about it. Don't think."

I opened the drawer of the bedside table and took out the envelope with the Interference Powder. There was still some left from my last attempt at fixing things. I carried it to my desk, turned on the light, and got out a piece of paper and a pencil. I want to sing, I thought. That wasn't so terrible! It wasn't like saying I wanted to be the prettiest girl in the world, or the richest, or even the luckiest. Hey, I wasn't even asking to be the best singer! All I wanted were a few lousy lessons. Well, good lessons. After all, I wanted to be a good singer.

And so I drew myself. I drew myself singing, my mouth open, the musical notes spilling out all over the page. This time I made sure not to cry. Then, before I could change my mind, I sprinkled Interference Powder over the page.

Don't think about it, I told myself. I closed my eyes so I wouldn't see the shimmer as the colors filled the air, and I jumped to my feet so I wouldn't feel the tiny shudder as the desk, drawing, and flakes of powder moved.

When it was safe and all was still again, I opened my eyes and funneled the Interference Powder back into its envelope, turned over the piece of paper on my desk, and got into bed, where I slept—suddenly, deeply, and without dreams, good or bad.

chapter thirteen

Morning.

I smelled bacon and heard it sputtering in the kitchen. My mom had made me a treat because today was the big day, the day I was supposed to become a fifth-grade Brain-Buster.

I looked at the clock. 7:05. In a minute I would hear, "Nina? You up?" and my day would begin. I closed my eyes.

Maybe I could be sick. I sat up in bed. I tried to swallow, willing my throat to be sore. It wasn't. I swung my legs out and hung them over the edge of the bed, looking at my bony knees.

Mysterious pains? Dizziness?

My mom clattered a pan down in the kitchen. I heard the rattle of a plate as she dragged it over another plate. Any second now, her voice.

Sudden blindness? Laryngitis?

"Nina?" my mom called from the bottom of the stairs. "You up?"

"I'm up," I sang out. My voice sounded almost cheerful.

"Breakfast in five," she said, and an instant later I heard her yank open the silverware drawer.

I got to my feet. A shower, I suddenly thought. Usually I had no time, but today I needed one to calm my nerves.

I went into the bathroom and turned on the faucet full force. Right away the little room began to fill with steam, and by the time I stepped into the tub, the mirror was fogged up. I tied up my hair in a scrunchy so it wouldn't get wet and stepped under the water. Instantly I felt a little bit better. I always liked hot showers. I liked to sing in them, and I decided to sing now, an old song that I loved for its totally slow pace and its long, low notes:

The water is wide, I can't cross o'er,
And neither I have wings to fly.
Give me a boat that can carry two,
And both shall row, my love and I.

My voice sounded great this morning, steady and sweet, and I was suddenly thrilled by it. I plunged on into the second verse:

Oh love is gentle and love is strong,
The sweetest flower when first it's new.
But love grows old and waxes cold,
And fades away like morning dew.

And that's when I remembered about the wish I had made the night before. *Stupid Nina!* I shouted, though not out loud. I closed my eyes and stuck my head under the stream of hot water, scrunchy and all.

Hadn't I learned that Interference Powder never worked out the way it was supposed to? Sure, singing lessons might have seemed like a great idea in the middle of the night, but right now, in the clear light of day, all I felt was panic.

Surely something was going to go really wrong this time, too. The only mystery was what it would be.

How could I have been such a jerk?

Beyond the pound of the shower, I heard the bathroom door open. I pulled open the shower curtain and saw my mom's face leaning into the room.

"Oh," she said. "I wondered what was taking you so long."

I smiled weakly.

"Look, Nina," she spoke quickly, "I just got a call from one of my patients. She needs to see me right away, so I have to go wait for her in the office. I'm so sorry this had to happen *this* morning."

Mom took a step closer.

"I wanted to sit with you for a bit downstairs," she said. "I know you're nervous, but I also know you're going to be great. Win or lose," she said. "It doesn't matter in the slightest. I'm so pleased that you're doing so well. You should just enjoy yourself today, right?"

I nodded, my throat suddenly thick. I knew if I spoke I'd surely burst into tears.

"So go get 'em, Nina." My mother grinned. She leaned forward, her hair catching a bit of spray from the shower, and kissed me.

"You all right?"

I nodded again.

"Okay. I'll be here when you get home. I want to hear all the details, so don't forget anything."

She turned and disappeared out the door. When it closed behind her, the room steamed up again, and I immediately gave in and cried.

Then I pulled myself together. I got out of the shower and dressed and pulled my wet hair into a ponytail. (Maybe I would get lucky, I thought, and catch a bad cold on the walk to school, and the school nurse would send me straight home.) Downstairs, I looked at the nice breakfast my mom had left for me—three strips of bacon next to a poached egg—all cold by now. I had no appetite for either, but I didn't want Mom to find them later, scraped into the garbage, so I ate everything in quick, tasteless bites. I washed my plate and put it in the dishwasher. I stepped into the mudroom to get my parka and heard the sharp, urgent sound of a strange voice through my mom's office wall and then my mother, responding in her Voice of Concern. I suddenly wished my mom would open her office door and come give me a huge, warm hug. *Fix it*, I thought, feeling miserable as I stood on the other side of the wall from her, hearing the muffled sound of her comforting somebody else. *Make it better. Make it go away, or at least back to where it was before.*

But, of course, she did nothing of the kind. And after a minute I pulled myself together, zipped up my parka, and set off down Wilton Street to meet my totally miserable fate.

chapter fourteen

Brain-Busters Extravaganza—Today!
read a huge red sign just inside the entryway. Kids were
clapping me on the back and whispering "Good luck!"
as I made my way along the corridor. I grinned as
bravely as I could and gave them all a thumbs-up. I was
just hanging up my parka when I noticed a pink carnation in the cubbyhole where I stow my backpack. There
was a little note attached to the stem with a red ribbon.
I bent down to read it: "Good luck, Nina. From Theo."

I felt my face flush a little. I shoved the flower deep
into my backpack and went on into the classroom.

The extravaganza was scheduled for first thing after
attendance. At least I wouldn't have to suffer with dread
all day long. Ms. Tulane did the roll call and then
instructed us to walk quietly down to the auditorium,
where Ms. Dravid's and Mrs. Hampshire's classes were
already seated. Behind us the grades kindergarten
through four filed in, everybody chattering at once. The
big room roared with voices. I closed my eyes and took
a ragged breath, imagining all of the eyes on me; and
as I did, I felt my teacher's hand on my shoulder.

"Why don't you go on up," she said kindly. "You might as well. Ms. Dravid's student is there already, I see."

I glanced up and saw three ordinary classroom seats on the near side of the podium. In one of them sat Theo, looking uncomfortably out over the masses of bobbing heads.

I nodded and began to move forward.

"Have fun," she chirped.

Sure, I thought.

I made my way over to the steps at the edge of the auditorium stage. As I reached them, Isobel fell into line in front of me, and my heart gave a sudden lurch. She was wearing her pink sweater and blue jeans and the green string of beads around her neck—the exact same clothes I'd drawn her in when I drew that picture of her onstage, as our class Brain-Buster! Maybe everything was going to be all right after all! Maybe the Interference Powder had worked, and it was Isobel heading for that chair beside Theo. But just as I thought that, Isobel turned right, away from Theo, and crossed the stage. My spirits sank again.

Isobel's assigned place was at one of the three desks lined up on the far side of the stage, facing the three seats where the Brain-Busters sat.

One of those seats is for me, I thought with resignation. There was no way around it: I was a Brain-Buster.

I crossed the stage and sat down next to Theo, and he gave me a watery grin. "Ready to rock 'n' roll?"

I shrugged uncomfortably. I wanted to thank him for his flower; but I thought that might embarrass him, so I said nothing. In another minute Ella came and sat on the other side of me. I wondered if Theo had given her a carnation too.

I didn't like to look out at the teeming auditorium, and I didn't like to look at where Isobel was sitting with two other girls, so I sat in my wooden chair looking at my hands and trying to remember something—anything—about life in New Amsterdam. On either side of me, Theo and Ella seemed to be doing the exact same thing, because none of us spoke. And then the audience went quiet. Mr. Arthur, our principal and the genius who'd thought up the Brain-Busters Extravaganza, approached the podium with a dumb grin stretched across his face.

"Welcome!" he said. "Welcome! Well, it's finally here: our very first Brain-Busters Extravaganza!"

Pause for applause, I said silently, and so he did as everyone clapped.

"Now we have three fine students representing their fifth-grade classes," he boomed. "And I would like to introduce them to you. Theo Matza is representing Ms. Dravid's class. Stand up, Theo!" And Theo stood. "Then Ella Serious, from Mrs. Hampshire's." Ella stood without having to be asked. Theo, unsure of whether he was supposed to remain on his feet, quickly sat down. "And finally, from Ms. Tulane's class, here is Nina Zabin."

I got up, my feet shaky, and gave a little wave before collapsing back down.

"Now, as you know," our principal continued, "the fifth grade has been immersed in the study of life in New Amsterdam for the past several weeks, and so we've decided to make that study the subject of this first Brain-Busters Extravaganza. Our fifth graders"—here he indicated with one pudgy hand the row of desks where Isobel was sitting between two other girls—"have been busy conjuring up questions for the contestants. Hope they're not too hard!" he said cheerily, and I heard a rumble of laughter from the seats out there, even as my stomach erupted in butterflies. He quickly introduced the girls, and there was polite applause for Isobel and for the other two, Lily and June, who strangely enough both had the same last name—Rosen—but weren't even related. "And now . . ." Mr. Arthur paused. "Where is that thing?" he asked his assistant, Ms. Songa, who was sitting in the first row. "Where did we put that thing?"

Ms. Songa was the kind of assistant who always knew what an expression like "that thing" meant. She got to her feet and climbed up the side of the stage. Then she went into one of the wings and retrieved what looked like a big fishbowl, only instead of fish, this bowl was filled with folded white papers. She set it squarely before Isobel. "These are our questions," he observed, stating the obvious. "Each of our experts will pick at random from the . . ." He trailed off, looking for the word he wanted.

The thing? I thought helpfully.

"From this," he concluded. "They may get one of their own class's questions or one from a different class. And they will then ask the question of their own class's Brain-Buster. If a Brain-Buster should fail to answer three questions correctly, he or she will be out of the competition. So!" He grinned at the audience. "Are you ready?"

Insane applause from the kindergartners.

"Are you ready?" This was directed at the panel, who nodded eagerly.

He turned to Theo, Ella and me. "How 'bout you?" He was trying for a friendly har-har tone.

"Sure are!" Theo said, and I didn't mind that he was speaking for me.

"Well then, let's begin!"

Mr. Arthur took his seat in the front row, and the girl beside Isobel, Theo's classmate from Ms. Dravid's class, got to her feet and leaned over Isobel to pluck a folded paper from the fish bowl. Quickly, she smoothed it out and read in a mumbled voice directed at her own feet.

"Speak up, Lily!" Ms. Dravid called from the third row.

"Oh, okay," she said, and read in a louder voice: "When did Peter Stuyvesant lose his leg?"

Ella, Theo, and I all looked at one another. Then, at the same instant, we all laughed. Ella covered her mouth as she giggled, and Theo was grinning. Even I had to admit that the question did a totally great job of cutting the tension.

The experts, I noticed, were glancing at one another,

too; but unlike us, they didn't really understand why the question was funny. Theo stood up.

"Well, at the time," he said, trying to keep a straight face, "some of the schoolchildren believed he had stepped into a rabbit hole, and the leg had been bitten off by the rabbit!" He looked down at me and Ella. I saw Ms. Tulane, in the second row, frown in confusion. Beside me, Ella's shoulders shook with laughter. "But the actual truth is that he lost it when he was the governor of Curaçao, which was a Dutch colony in the West Indies."

Lily, Theo's classmate, looked to their teacher in some confusion. "That's right," she said. "I mean, not the part about the rabbit. The other part."

"Okay," she answered. "You can sit down, Lily."

Lily sat down.

The other girl got to her feet. This was June, from Mrs. Hampshire's class. Back in second grade, June had sat at the desk behind me and pelted me with rubber erasers. Contrary to what you might think, a rubber eraser can really hurt if it's thrown hard enough.

Ella stood up, her hands clasped together in front of her. June selected her question and cleared her throat.

"Name three things that were typical of the Dutch houses in New Amsterdam."

"Okay." Ella looked at the auditorium ceiling. "Well, there was the chimney. It had steps so you could climb up to clean it. That's one." She glanced at Mrs. Hampshire, who sat beside the principal, and Mrs.

Hampshire nodded kindly. "And the doors were Dutch doors. I mean, we call them Dutch doors today. The top and bottom opened separately, so you could let in the breeze through the top half while the bottom half stayed shut to keep the animals from wandering into the house. And . . . um, there would be tiles around the fireplaces. Blue-and-white tiles that came from Holland. I guess they reminded the Dutch settlers of home. I mean, their old home, before they came to the New World."

"Very nice, Ella!" said Mrs. Hampshire softly, and Ella smiled and sat down in obvious relief.

Now it was my turn. I stood, my hands clammy at my sides. Across the stage, Isobel was avoiding my gaze. She rummaged in the bowl, feeling for the right slip of paper with her fingers, as if they possessed the ability to read the question for her, and finally drew out a piece. I gazed at it numbly and took a deep breath.

"Oh," Isobel said as she read to herself. I wondered if that meant the question was one she'd thought up or if it was new to her. "Can you describe a song that schoolchildren in New Amsterdam might have sung?"

A song! That had never come up in our study sessions! I concentrated. The Dutch in New Amsterdam weren't that big on music, apart from singing hymns at church. Then, slowly, I began to remember one of our first lessons about the colony in which Ms. Tulane told us how the Dutch hadn't always gotten along with the English settlers in New England. They'd made fun of them by calling them "Jonker," which was actually pronounced "Yonker," meaning a country squire, and "Doodle," which meant a fool; and they sang this song about their English neighbors. Over the next couple of hundred years, it turned into "Yankee Doodle." I frowned, trying to remember the version of the song they would have known in the colony, and then it came to me. And without really thinking about it, I opened my mouth and sang:

> *Jonker doodle came to town*
> *In his strip-ed trousers,*
> *Couldn't see the town because*
> *There were so many houses.*

But now, this is the really amazing thing. While I was singing, I looked out over the auditorium and saw people with their mouths dropped open. I thought: What are they looking at? Or actually, What are they listening to? What is making them look so astonished? It's only me, singing "Yankee Doodle Dandy"! I mean, I know it's a little surprising that I would sing the song instead of just saying, "They sang a song that was going to turn into 'Yankee Doodle Dandy,'" but it's not crazy or anything. Somebody asks you about a song, and you hum a few bars, right? To show them how the song goes. So what's the big deal?

The big deal, I realized, even as I belted out the tune, was how I sounded singing "Yankee Doodle Dandy." I sounded GREAT.

Not perfectly fine, not even in tune, but GREAT.

I had never heard myself sing this way, except perhaps a little bit in the shower earlier that morning. But this was different, I realized as I finished the last line of the tune. This was . . .

Oh no. This was Interference Powder!

There was a wave of loud applause. I felt behind me for my chair and sat down. I heard Ella's voice near my ear. "Nina! That was wonderful!"

Across the stage Isobel sat motionless, the paper still in her hand. Suddenly, she turned to Mr. Arthur. "Yes, that's the right answer."

"She didn't have to sing it, though!" Drea Wells shouted from the audience.

"No, but isn't it nice that she did?" the principal said cheerily. "Next question!"

I sat with my face warm and growing warmer. Something was not right, something I couldn't quite put my finger on and wasn't sure I wanted to. Something unexpected, something awful, something about to reveal itself was nagging at me. I couldn't say what it was; but in a strange, almost sickening way, it began to dawn on me. I knew it by the way I'd just sounded when I sang the song. And I knew it because I remembered how I had opened my mouth to say, in a perfectly civilized tone of voice, the words "Yankee Doodle Dandy" but instead the song itself had come out.

Theo correctly answered a question about the first Dutch ship to arrive in America and what it was doing

there (the *Half Moon*, captained by the Englishman
Henry Hudson, in search of the northwest passage),
and Ella rose to report on the purchase of Manhattan
island (from the Algonquin Indians, by Peter Minuit, for
roughly twenty-four dollars in beads, ornaments, col-
ored cloth, blankets, and knives).

"Not a bad deal!" our principal said, chortling. "I
think we may be here all night before one of our Brain-
Busters misses a question! Luckily, we've got plenty of
questions left!" He looked at me. "Ready, Ms. Zabin?"

Barely aloud, I said these words: "I'm ready."

And then I knew for sure what the awful thing was.
Because I didn't say those three words at all.

I sang them.

Like a little song of three notes, low then higher, then
back to the first: *"I'm-red-dy!"*

I knew for sure, because I had not set out to sing
those words, but to say them like a normal person: "I'm
ready." And they had come out as singing.

I put my hands over my mouth, clamping shut my
lips as if I could keep the song inside.

"Ms. Zabin? Are you all right?"

I concentrated. This was ridiculous! If I tried to
speak then speak I would. I would say the word
certainly. I would say it without an ounce of melody
to it, and I would do it right now.

"Certainly!" I sang. Three more musical steps, these
going up in regular steps, like a scale: *Cer-tan-lee!*

"Well, all right then!" he said, looking a little puzzled.

"It's your turn."

Utterly horrified, I got to my feet. I had wanted to sing and sing I obviously could. But I could no longer do anything else. Speak! Shout! Whisper! All gone, and if my past adventures with Interference Powder were anything to go by, then gone for good. How would I communicate with people? How would I chat on the phone? How would I call operator assistance? How would I go into a restaurant and ask for a hamburger and a chocolate shake? How would I ever talk to my mom across the kitchen table?

When I thought of this last thing, my throat began to tighten with tears. Oh great! I thought. What a way to make an absolutely horrendous situation even worse! I will not cry, I told myself fiercely. I will not under any circumstances and despite threat of torture and death . . . CRY!

So naturally I felt the first tear begin to run down my cheek even before Isobel reached into the *thing*.

"Your question," she said calmly, her eyes on the paper, "is: What, apart from the Dutch Reformed Church, were some of the other religions that existed in New Amsterdam?"

Oh, I thought, there were Lutherans and Quakers and the shipwrecked Jews from Brazil who arrived in 1654 and stayed to become the very first Jewish Americans. But, of course, there was a world of difference between thinking this and saying it aloud. The worrying I had done over whether I'd know the answers in the Brain-Busters Extravaganza seemed very far away now. Of course, I knew the answers! I'd been silly to dread such a little thing as getting an answer wrong. Now I had far more scary things to worry about, and believe me, I was worrying about them.

"Do you need more time?" Isobel asked. Was I imagining it or did her voice sound just a little bit kind?

What I needed, and desperately, was to find a way not to open my mouth. But I couldn't think of one. I shook my head.

There were two choices, as I saw them. One, I could run off the auditorium stage, up the aisle, down the corridor, out the door, and across the neighborhood, all the way home to Wilton Street. This would make me look like a complete and utter moron.

Two, I could try to speak my answer. After all, I couldn't be absolutely and totally sure what would happen. I could be wrong about this singing thing. Maybe my nerves were somehow involved, right? And even if I humiliated myself by singing the words, it wouldn't be any more humiliating than running away.

Which should I do? I opened my mouth. *"There were Lutherans!"* my voice sang out. *"There were Quakers and Jews!"*

I stopped. It was terrible. This time it was no three-note jingle—it was a full-fledged aria. My soaring tones echoed through the silent room, and for one long moment, I stared at the startled, focused gazes of hundreds of pairs of eyes. Then, abruptly, one loud laugh split the silence and immediately everyone was laughing. Laughter, loud and ragged, sputtering and low and shrieking and endless. I stood, unable to budge.

Across the stage, Isobel said sharply: "The answer is correct."

"Yeah, but like I said, *she didn't have to sing it,*" Drea jeered.

"Shut up, Drea," said Isobel, and amid my fog of humiliation I noticed that she'd stopped being mad at me long enough to defend me. I looked over at her and she stood up. The room, still vibrating with laughter, blurred all around me, and the only thing I could see clearly at all was Isobel. She came around her desk and took a step toward me. Then she took another step.

"Nina?" she said softly. "You okay?"

I was afraid to try to speak, so I just shook my head. No, I wasn't okay.

"Can you talk?"

I couldn't talk. That was the whole point.

"You want me to get them to call your mom?"

My mom! And what would my mom think about this? I would have to tell her everything: about my ill-gotten perfect score, the wrong I'd done Isobel, my newfound singing talent. And how would I explain that I'd never ever open my mouth again for fear of sounding like a one-person opera? And even worse, my singing lessons! I might as well kiss that dream goodbye. Forever!

"Nina?" Isobel said again, this time touching me on the shoulder; and when she did, something else happened. I felt the tears come so quickly, there was no way I could stop them. They were suddenly just there, on my cheeks, in my eyes, even—it seemed—down my neck, a salty waterfall; and all at once I was a blubbering Brain-Buster, bawling at center stage. The tears slipped through my fingers and coated my face, and then—as if from a great distance—I was aware of one tear hitting the floor.

Splat!

Which was when the next incredible thing happened.

A bubble of water squirted up from under the stage as if to meet my tear as it sank down between the boards. It sprouted like a little spring: *blub, blub, blub*. And then there was more water—a hiss, not a bubble—and suddenly the water shot straight into the air, like a geyser in Yellowstone Park. *Whoosh!* It went high over my head, hitting the ceiling and taking everyone's attention away from me. Isobel, her hand still on my shoulder, yanked me back.

"Golly!" I heard her say. We were both getting soaked by the shooting water. "What on earth?"

But of course I knew what on earth. I knew it was my tear that had caused this. Not my tear here onstage only a moment earlier, but the tear I had cried over Isobel's picture, after I had sprinkled it with Interference Powder. That tear had made a flood, and the flood had erupted right here at center stage, just where the tear had fallen on the page.

Mr. Arthur, bounding up the stage steps, came hurtling over to us. Pushing us aside, he stood precisely where we had stood, gazing at the water with wonder. Finally, regaining a few of his senses, he shouted to the teachers to clear the auditorium and to Ms. Songa to find Sitney, who was our custodian, and get him here quick; and in the chaos that followed, I slipped away from Isobel and found my way out of the building. I ran all the way home, crept upstairs to my room, and sat stonily on my bed, waiting for the rest of my life to fall apart.

chapter fifteen

Forty-five minutes later, my mom flung open my door and rushed into the room. "Oh, thank goodness," she said frantically. "I didn't know where you were! The *school* doesn't know where you are! They just called me and said it's like you disappeared off the face of the earth. Nina!" She sounded suddenly furious. "What got into you? Why didn't you tell somebody you were going home? Why didn't you call me? Didn't you think about how scared I'd be?"

Miserable, I shrugged.

"Well, that's not much of an answer," my mom said. And then she softened. "Nina, did that quiz thing maybe not go so great?"

I stared at her for a minute, then I nodded.

She came into the room and sat on my bed. "Want to talk about it?"

Boy, did I want to talk about it! That, unfortunately, was the whole problem.

"Want to tell me what happened?" she tried again when I kept silent.

I sniffled. Then I took a deep breath. After all, it had

to happen sometime. I couldn't stay quiet forever.

"There's something wrong with my voice," I sang. It came out softly and low, like a funeral hymn or something, and she stared at me.

"What did you say?" my mother asked.

"I didn't say!" My voice soared. *"I sang. I can only sing now. I want to speak but it comes out singing. I'm not doing it on purpose!"* I finished with a trill of outrage in a high soprano. For a weird moment I stopped to think, Hey! I didn't know I could reach such a high note—cool!

My mother, on the other hand, was staring at me.

"I tried to answer the questions," I went on, and this time it sounded like a merry little folk song. *"But when I start to speak, my voice doesn't do what I tell it to. Please don't be mad at me."*

Mom took a deep breath. "I'm many things right now, Nina, but mad at you isn't one of them." She paused. "When did you realize that you were having this . . . this problem? Can I ask you that?"

I looked guiltily at the drawer of my bedside table. *"When I answered the first question. But it was a song. The question was about a song, and so I sang the song. But even so I felt like there was something wrong. And the next question, I tried to answer it and it came out . . ."* I looked at her perplexed expression. What was I doing? What made me think she would ever be able to understand, for all her trying. *"I can't talk!"* I wailed. This time I sounded tuneful but hoarse. *"I can't talk! I'm never going to be able to talk again!"*

My mom shook her head. "Oh, my sweetie." She hugged me. "Oh, that's not true," she crooned in her Voice of Concern. "I'm sure a good rest will put this all to rights. I know how nervous you were about that Brain-Busters thing. You've just gotten yourself all worked up, and you'll be fine. Trust me. I've seen lots of people who get in all sorts of fixes from plain old worry."

I shrugged, feeling terrible. I was far from confident myself.

"Here's my advice," she said brightly. "Let's just relax, the two of us. I'll cancel my appointments for this afternoon. We'll go to the movies, okay?"

I nodded eagerly. This was an unexpected development. My mom had never in her life canceled patients to take me to the movies.

"What about school?" I sang.

"Oh, school." She shrugged. "It's out. They had some kind of plumbing crisis over there. They've sent everybody home. Can you imagine?" I smiled weakly. "One little leak in the auditorium and everybody's hysterical. You'd think they could just find a bucket or something and get on with the school day."

"I guess." Two notes. Two little staccato notes. Middle C by the sound of them.

"All right then." She smiled. "Why don't you change your clothes?" She nodded at them, still damp from the geyser under the auditorium stage.

"Would you like to go to the movies?"

"Yes!" I trilled. "I'd love to! But is it really okay? I mean, for you to cancel your patients?"

She gazed at me with a Major League Look of Concern. "It isn't nothing," my mom agreed. "But yes, it's okay."

This made me sniffle a bit, and for a moment I thought I might let loose again; but I managed to choke down the tears by thinking of burst pipes and buckets overflowing. I had to hand it to my mom, though. That Look of Concern? It always got to me.

I stood up, changed my clothes, and waited for Mom to make her phone calls to her patients. Then we climbed into the car and drove to the New York Deli and ordered hamburgers and milk shakes. Mom read me a letter from my aunt Sally, which she had swiped from the mailbox as we pulled out of our drive. Aunt Sally had just returned from her retreat, and she wrote that she was feeling calmer than she had in years. For the first time she was asking herself the question: *What do I love to do?*

"I hope *you'll* find something you love to do," Mom said, stirring her milk shake with the straw. "And then I hope you'll find a way to make a living at it. That's the trick."

I sighed and took a bite of my half-sour pickle. Finding a way to make a living at what I loved to do was not exactly at the forefront of my thoughts just now. Finding a way to say "Which way to the ladies' room, please?" or "Would you kindly remove the poisonous snake that's underneath my bed?" was more my current concern.

I couldn't tell her those things, so I just nodded and kept my mouth shut.

It was easy to keep silent at the movie, of course. My mom even bought the popcorn and soda so I wouldn't have to sing, *"A large popcorn and two Cokes, please!"* to what I'm sure would have been a very surprised person at the concession counter.

When we got home, there was a message on our answering machine that the plumbing problem had been fixed and school would be open in the morning. There was also a nice message from Ella Serious asking me if I was all right and saying the whole Brain-Busters thing had been canceled because of the pipe bursting. And there was a message from my teacher, Ms. Tulane, wondering if my mom would give her a call.

"Hmm," Mom said, coming up beside me to listen to this last message. She gave me a look that said *You want to run upstairs and not listen to me as I make this call, don't you?*

I climbed the stairs to my room and sat on my bed, listening to her mumble into the phone to my teacher. Then I heard her pulling a chair out from the kitchen table as she settled in for a lengthy conversation, and then nothing more until, nearly a half hour later, she came upstairs to find me.

"What about dinner?" Mom asked. "I have some

lasagna in the freezer, or we can have the lamb chops I picked up yesterday."

I grinned bravely, struggling not to ask about her conversation with Ms. Tulane. *"Lamb chops!"* I sang out. *"You know how much I love them!"*

It came out sounding like a jingle on a TV commercial: *Lamb Chops! Lamb Chops! How I love them! How I love them!*

I looked over at the doorway. She was standing there, her face pale, her arms at her sides. It took her a minute to find her own voice.

"This may be more serious than I thought," my mother said.

chapter sixteen

Next morning, to my surprise, Mom didn't even try to get me up for school. This was a relief since I'd been lying in bed for nearly an hour, rehearsing my arguments in case she tried to make me go. (*"No!"* my mind voice soared. *"I will not go!"*) The minute hand clicked past 7:00, then 7:30, and made its way on to 8:00. I heard Mom moving around the kitchen, and I smelled coffee as it began to drip through the coffeemaker.

I turned over and groaned, and even my groan sounded totally like singing, which made me feel, if it was possible, even worse. Maybe I should enter a religious order of silence on some mountain in the Alps, like Maria in *The Sound of Music*; but then I remembered how Maria was always singing, which got her into trouble with the other nuns, and I groaned again. Or instead of silence, I could try to find a community of men and women who were constantly bursting into song: *"We're out of toilet paper!"* *"Not spinach again!"*—but just thinking about it made me feel a little sick.

Oh, how I wanted to talk! To whisper, to chatter, to orate or yell. How dumb I'd been to take it all for granted.

Now, even the chance to whine or complain like a normal person seemed enviable. But it was pointless to long for what I couldn't have. Interference Powder had never changed its mind about anything yet, and there was no reason to think it would change its mind about this. I was done for. And if my mom thought she was going to get me through the doors of Riverside School ever again, for any reason whatsoever, she was totally mistaken.

I was thinking about this so hard that I didn't hear her climb the stairs.

"Up we get, Nina." Her voice interrupted my thoughts, annoyingly cheerful. "Time to get dressed."

I sat up in bed and sang, with some outrage, *"But I'm not going to school! I won't! I won't!"*

"No, you won't," she said, coming in and sitting on the bed. "Not today."

"Not ever!" My voice soared high.

"Not today," she corrected. "But you still have to get up. We have an appointment."

Oh no, I thought. I didn't know what she had planned, but it had to be something foul. Speech therapist? Pediatrician?

"Who?" The single syllable, I noted, sounded almost normal.

"Someone who can help. That's all you need to know right now." She got up, pointed at my bureau, and said, "Five minutes. Dress casual."

This was her attempt at humor, I thought. As if I would dress any other way.

So I put on a black shirt and a pair of jeans. By the time I had brushed my teeth and my hair and made my way downstairs, my mom had on her coat and was standing by the back door, looking impatient.

"We don't have time for breakfast," she said.

"That's okay," I told her. It sounded like a low, mournful song. *"I'm not hungry, anyway."*

"Poor sweetie," she cooed. "Now let's go."

I got in the car, and we pulled out onto Wilton Street. The branches were letting loose their brown leaves, littering the sidewalk with crunchy, feathery piles that, in other years, Isobel and I had raked into heaps and rolled in.

Our appointment turned out to be in a little red brick office building just off Witherspoon with a collection of brass nameplates out front. It happened to be my dentist's building, and I eyed my mom as we parked in the familiar lot in back.

"Dr. Patel?" I sang. *"How do you think she's going to help?"*

"Not Dr. Patel," said my mom. "I don't see this as a teeth issue."

Well, at least we agree about that, I thought sourly. I got out of the car.

She went to the front door, and I followed her inside. The hall looked sort of homey for an office building. You could see that it had once been a family house and somebody had come along and chopped it into smaller offices. When we climbed the stairs, I imagined somebody climbing upstairs to his or her bedroom. Maybe that person had lounged in bed in the room in which I had my cavities filled. We kept climbing all the way to the former attic, and I puffed my way up the third flight of stairs. There, on the landing, was a single door. And on that door was a plaque. And written on that plaque were the words: Child Psychology.

"Oh no!" I wailed, forgetting that I had vowed never to sing in public again. *"You're not taking me to a therapist!"*

"Calm yourself, Nina," my mother said quietly.

"You think this is in my mind?" I half hissed, half sang.

"I think you need to talk to someone," she answered. "And I think that someone isn't me."

"That someone is no one," I told her, my voice frantic but still, unfortunately, singsongy. *"Please don't make me."*

"I'm not *making* you, Nina. But I wouldn't have brought you here if I didn't think he could help."

He! I thought. Even *worse!*

But that was nothing compared to what happened next. My mother stepped up to the door and knocked, three crisp knocks, and I heard a shuffle from beyond. One muffled footstep, then another, and the brass doorknob turned. The door swung into a dim office, brushing against dark carpeting, to reveal a bright pink painting, obviously by a child, framed on the white wall. There was a window overlooking the house next door and an old wooden desk with a girl's photograph on top of it. I knew that girl. That girl was Ella Serious, and the man standing with his hand on the door was her father.

chapter seventeen

"Welcome!" Dr. Serious said with a big smile.

I looked at him in amazement. Then I looked at my mom. She didn't really expect me to talk to Dr. Serious, did she?

"Hello," she said. "You remember Nina."

"But of course." He grinned at me. "How are you today, Nina?"

I simply glared at him. Then I turned to my mother and gave her a look that said ARE YOU NUTS?

"Come on, Nina." She sighed. "Nobody's going to bite you."

"That's right," Dr. Serious agreed. "I haven't bitten a patient since my first year on the job. They said if I did it again they'd have my license, and I need my license."

That caught me off guard. I looked at the two armchairs in the room. Which one was supposed to be for me?

"Serena," he said suddenly, "why don't you wait outside? Nina and I will have a talk, and you'll be right there if we need you. How about that?"

"All right with me," she said pleasantly. "Okay by you, Nina?"

I grabbed her sleeve and pulled her down till her ear was against my mouth. *"I can't talk to him!"* I hissed. *"I mean, I can't sing to him! I'm too embarrassed!"*

My mother considered. Then she whispered back, "How about paper? I could get you some paper, and you could write down what you want to say."

I thought about that. It did seem like a good solution. Leaving immediately and going to breakfast at P.J.'s Pancake House sounded like a totally better solution, but if we couldn't do that . . . *"Okay,"* I whispered.

My mom looked over at the desk, where Dr. Serious was watching us, a little half-smile on his face. "Would it be all right if Nina used your legal pad?" my mother asked. "She would prefer to write down her half of the conversation."

"Certainly," he answered, as if that were a common request. He handed me the pad, then gave me a black ballpoint pen.

"I'll be outside," said my mom. And then she left us alone in the little room, clicking shut the door behind her.

For a long minute I just looked around, since I was a little too shy to look at Ella's dad. There was a skylight overhead, which showed one long branch of a tree and a lot of gray sky. There was a bookcase against one wall full of books with titles such as *Evaluating the Adolescent* and *Puberty in the American Male* and *Preadolescence: Staging Ground for Adulthood*. Fun reading, I thought. It was getting pretty quiet in the room.

"So, Nina," Dr. Serious said suddenly. "What's going on?"

What's going on? I thought. I picked up my pen and wrote, then turned the pad around to show him: WHAT DO YOU MEAN?

He smiled. "Your mom says you're having a problem with your voice."

I gave him an exaggerated shrug and wrote: NO PROBLEM!

"No problem? You think it's normal to be talking to me on paper?"

Well, it was hard to argue with that. So I changed the subject and wrote: WHY YOU? WHY DID MY MOM BRING ME HERE?

"Oh." He sat back in his seat. "Well, I work with kids. That is, I'm a therapist specializing in children. Your mother thought I might be able to help."

WELL, SHE WAS WRONG, I wrote. YOU CAN'T HELP.

He seemed to consider this very seriously. "How can you be sure? Maybe I've seen a hundred kids with the exact same problem, and they're all talking flawlessly today. Maybe I've helped kids with even more serious problems than yours. You could give me a try. Can't hurt, right?"

I looked glumly at him and shook my head. Then I thought of something funny. SERIOUS PROBLEMS? I scribbled. CALL DR. SERIOUS!

But to my surprise, he didn't smile when I showed it to him.

"Dr. what?" He looked at me in confusion. Then, as if finally understanding, he said, "You think my name is 'Serious'?"

Now I was the one to be surprised. I wrote: YOU'RE ELLA'S DAD. ELLA SERIOUS.

And when he read this, he threw back his head and roared. I just sat there, feeling smaller and smaller in my seat. Why was he laughing at me? Therapists aren't supposed to laugh! I never heard my mother laugh in her office at the back of our house.

"Not Serious, Nina! Not S-E-R-I-O-U-S! My name is—"

And he said his name. It sounded like "serious," but I could tell by the way he pronounced it that it wasn't S-E-R-I-O-U-S.

I wrote "SERIES." LIKE TV SERIES?

"No." He was still laughing. "Not S-E-R-I-E-S. It's—"

And he said the name again. Then he spelled it.

"C-E-R-E-S. The word was Roman, originally. Ceres was a goddess. She was the Roman version of the Greek goddess Demeter. You know about Demeter, right?"

Demeter. I concentrated. Demeter was the goddess of the harvest. When her daughter, Persephone, was kidnapped by the lord of the underworld, she went into mourning—that was winter. And when her daughter came back to her for six months every year, it was summer. I knew about Demeter. I nodded.

"And Ceres is where the word *cereal* comes from. Did you know that?"

I didn't know that. I shook my head.

"You thought our name was 'Serious'?" He grinned. "Well, I suppose that's perfectly understandable. They do sound almost exactly alike. And you probably never saw Ella's name written down."

I wouldn't have, I thought, since she was in a different class.

I looked at him. He had finished laughing now and was only looking a little amused. I shrugged.

"So how did the Brain-Busters thing go? Ella said there was some kind of catastrophe with water all over the stage."

I nodded. Did he expect me to add something to that?

"But you know what?" he went on, settling back in his chair. "She also said she was relieved when the pipe burst, or whatever it was. She wasn't having fun." He paused. "Personally, I thought the whole thing was a bad idea. I don't think kids enjoy being put in a position where they're suddenly supposed to be representing their peers. Leaders emerge from a group naturally, you know? One kid will obviously be the fastest runner or a couple of kids will just consistently do well on math tests, and everyone knows that and adjusts to that. But when you have an adult come in and say, 'Boom! You're the best in the class; you represent everybody else!' it gets sticky. Who needs it? It's tough enough being a kid, right?"

I frowned at him. Then I wrote: SO WHY DIDN'T ELLA BACK OUT? OR WHY DIDN'T YOU TELL THE PRINCIPAL?

He nodded. "Two questions, two answers. She didn't back out because she didn't want to call attention to herself. And I didn't call the principal for the same reason: She didn't want me to. See, to her it came down to a choice between a bad situation and a worse situation. Plus, by then she had gotten to know you and Theo a little better, so for her that was kind of like the silver lining. And she didn't want to upset the boat for the two of you just because she wasn't that gung ho on the idea."

I nodded. I knew just how Ella felt. And probably, Theo had felt the same way, too.

"But Ella told me something else," he went on, looking up at the ceiling as if it were suddenly fascinating. "She said you got asked a question about a song, and you sang the song. She said you have an absolutely beautiful singing voice."

I blushed.

"Is singing something you're interested in?"

I sighed. Singing was something I *used* to be interested in. Now all I was interested in was never singing again.

"Do you feel that you have a talent for singing?" asked Dr. Ceres.

It was a hard question to answer. After a minute I

took my pen and wrote: I HAVE A GOOD VOICE, BUT I KNOW IT COULD BE BETTER. THAT'S WHY I WANTED TO TAKE SINGING LESSONS.

He leaned forward slightly to read what I'd written. "Singing lessons?" He frowned.

I wrote: I USED TO ASK MY MOM IF I COULD TAKE SINGING LESSONS. BUT SHE SAID NO.

"Why was that?" He sat back in his seat.

I bent over the pad. SHE THOUGHT IT WOULD TAKE TIME AWAY FROM MY SCHOOLWORK.

"Was that so important? You seem to be doing just fine in school."

I shook my head and wrote: NOT ALL THAT GREAT. THE BRAIN-BUSTERS THING WAS KIND OF A FLUKE.

"Really?" He seemed interested. "What kind of a fluke?"

Well, I was hardly going to tell him what kind of a fluke, so I just shrugged. Then I wrote: MY FRIEND ISOBEL IS REALLY SMART. SHE CAN DO HER HOMEWORK IN A FEW MINUTES. I HAVE TO SPEND HOURS ON THE SAME STUFF, AND I NEVER DO AS WELL AS SHE DOES.

"You're not smart?" He looked at me intently. "Oh, I beg to differ, Nina. I didn't need to be told you were an official Brain-Buster to know you were smart. I knew that ten seconds after I met you. If you don't always ace every test or every assignment at school, I can assure you, it has nothing to do with how smart you are."

I couldn't help myself. I blushed again.

"Besides, people are smart in different ways, you know."

I didn't know, so I just looked at him.

"Somebody can be a scientific genius and be incapable of putting a sentence together. Another person can have difficulty memorizing facts but be amazingly intuitive when it comes to other people. There are brilliant writers who couldn't add two plus two if their life depended on it. History is full of creative minds that have changed the world. And what about the artists?"

This was like dangling bait in front of me. I wrote: WHAT ABOUT THE ARTISTS?

"Ah." Dr. Ceres grinned. "You ever hear about Jackson Pollock? Guy could barely tie his shoes. But one day in 1947 he went out to the garage behind his house and started dripping paint onto a canvas with a stick. Since then every single artist in the world has had to reckon with him and his genius."

I frowned. I was pretty sure I knew which one Jackson Pollock was. Isobel's parents had lots of books about him.

"Robert Frost dropped out of two colleges. Did you know that? But he still managed to become one of our country's greatest poets."

I had to agree with that. I had always liked that poem about the man who comes to two roads in the woods and doesn't know which one to take.

"But like I said," Dr. Ceres smiled, "it isn't just artists. People are not gingerbread men. They're all different.

And don't forget, sometimes you can't tell right from the beginning how a person is going to turn out. Kids need time to discover their true selves and their true talents. Look at Albert Einstein! Einstein failed math class when he was a kid!"

I stared at him. People talked about Albert Einstein all the time in Princeton, because he lived here for a lot of his life and came up with many of his physics theories here. I'd never heard the part about his failing math class, though.

Dr. Ceres seemed to be considering something. He gave me a solemn look, but it wasn't quite a Look of Concern. It was more of a Look of Profound Wisdom. It didn't surprise me at all that the next thing out of his mouth sounded a lot like advice. "Let me tell you something, Nina. It's something I've learned from all the kids I've ever seen in my practice. Not to mention from my own daughter. Not to mention," he smiled, "from what I remember about my own childhood, hundreds of years ago."

I smiled at that, too.

"There are basically two things every kid needs to figure out before she or he can grow up. And it's not something they teach you in school, believe me."

Okay, I'll admit it. I was curious. I put up my hands to say "What?"

"She has to figure out what she wants out of life. Then she has to figure out who she is. It sounds easy, but it isn't easy."

I nodded my agreement. It did sound easy, but I knew it wasn't.

"There's a third thing, too," he said, sitting back in his chair. "But that comes later. After you know who you are and what you want out of life, you have to figure out what you have to offer the world. A person who answers all three of those questions, and then acts on the answers, will have lived a very good life." He sighed and shook his head. "But these are big ideas. I want to ask you something much more specific, okay?"

I nodded okay.

"Do you have any idea why you've stopped speaking?"

I stared at him. Didn't he know? Hadn't my mom told him what the problem was? Hadn't Ella told her dad that crazy Nina couldn't open her mouth without singing? Or was he just pretending not to know?

I wrote: EVERY TIME I TRY TO SAY SOMETHING IT COMES OUT SINGING. I CAN'T HELP IT. I WANT TO STOP, BUT I CAN'T. SO I'M NEVER GOING TO SPEAK ANOTHER WORD FOR THE REST OF MY LIFE.

And you can't make me, I added silently.

"Really!" He said, reading what I'd written. "How fascinating. And this just happened?"

I nodded.

"And do you have any idea why it should have happened?"

I shook my head quickly. If I wasn't going to tell my

own mother about Interference Powder, I certainly wasn't going to tell Dr. Ceres!

"And is this something you wanted to happen, Nina?"

Wanted to happen! I looked at him as if he were nuts. Who could want this miserable situation to happen? Did he actually think it was going to be easy for me, singing my way through life? Was that supposed to be *What I wanted out of life* and *Who I was* and *What I had to offer the world*?

I wrote in big black letters: NO! I HATE THIS! I DID NOT WANT THIS!

He nodded calmly as he read what I'd scrawled. Then he said, "Well, what do you want? Right now," and his voice was sort of soft and soothing. "Right now, today. What are the things you want most in your life? Can you write them for me?"

I looked down at my pad. I had pressed so hard with the ballpoint pen that the yellow paper had actually ripped, and I stared at what I'd written, feeling totally frustrated and helpless.

Dr. Ceres reached into a drawer. "Tell you what," he said. "Why don't we swap? I'd like to make a few notes on my pad. You can use a piece of this to write on if you want." He handed me a piece of his stationary: Dr. Brian Ceres, Adolescent Psychotherapy, 10 Hulfish Street, Princeton, New Jersey.

We traded, my torn yellow pad for his sheet of stationary.

Then he began writing, and I started to think. I was taking his question seriously. All of a sudden I wanted to answer it for myself.

Forget about Interference Powder, I thought. Forget about the Brain-Busters Extravaganza. Forget about Isobel and Theo and Ella and her dad. Forget about the burst water pipes and Ms. Charlemagne and life in New Amsterdam!

What did I want?

It wasn't that complicated, after all.

I started to write.

I WANT ISOBEL TO BE MY FRIEND AGAIN. I WANT MY MOM TO BE HAPPY. I DON'T WANT HER TO BE LONELY. I WANT MY AUNT SALLY TO FIND HER PASSION. I WANT ELLA TO BE MY FRIEND. I WANT THEO TO ASK ME TO GO TO THE MOVIES. I WANT TO KNOW THE PERSON I REALLY AM, DEEP DOWN, SO I CAN BE TRUE TO THAT PER-SON AND STOP WORRYING ABOUT THE THINGS I'M PROBABLY NEVER GOING TO BE VERY GOOD AT. I WOULD REALLY, REALLY, REALLY LIKE TO TAKE SINGING LESSONS.

When I had finished, I looked up, and I realized he had been watching me for a while. "All done?" he said.

I sang: *"All done."*

And then our session was done, too.

chapter eighteen

I wasn't cured, of course. But even so, I was sort of light-hearted as we drove home, past the trees with their wild, fiery colors and the sky a shocking blue.

My mother drove beside me, lost in thought. After my talk with Dr. Ceres—that is, after his talk with me—I had switched places with her, sitting in the corridor while she disappeared inside the office with him for a good half hour. When she came out, she hugged me and smiled. But I could tell she was distracted, and she stayed distracted as we crept through the traffic on Nassau Street.

She had patients of her own that afternoon, so I sat with her for a silent lunch of turkey sandwiches and tomato soup, then went upstairs to my room when the buzzer of her office door sounded. Darwin was curled up on my bed, a vibrating knot of gray fur. When he saw me, he stretched like the lazy soul he was and walked slowly off to find another soft place where there would be no humans to disturb him.

The afternoon had grown warm, and after the cold snap earlier in the week, my room felt stuffy. I opened the window, leaned my head out a bit, and felt the welcome breeze against my forehead. Fred was in the backyard next door, barking obnoxiously at a black squirrel high up in a pine tree, as if he thought he might be able to convince it to come down and be eaten. He'd never been able to catch that squirrel, but he just kept right on trying. *Give it up, Fred,* I thought, and I was about to shout at him when I remembered how the words would sound when they came out. I pulled my head inside.

It was now two o'clock. At school they'd be starting social studies: the American Revolution. I supposed I should read a few of the chapters in my history book, but my head was already too full of what I'd been talking about with Dr. Ceres, so I did what I always did when I felt jumpy and excited. I got out some paper and my watercolor paints and set them on my desk in front of the window.

For a while I painted the tree in the backyard next door, and the black squirrel high up in its branches, and then Fred down below, looking up with his teeth bared. I painted my mom, with a Look of Concern on her face. Then I decided to paint an exotic flower with a pink middle and great purple leaves, which left big puddles of purple watercolor on top of the desk. It wasn't the best work I'd ever done; but as I painted, I felt myself calm down a little, and my thoughts stopped racing and slowed to the point that I could start to sort them out.

The problem was that I understood so little about what had happened to me. There was a whole list of important stuff I just didn't know! For example, I didn't even know what Interference Powder actually *was*, or why it seemed to be able to . . . well, to *interfere* with everything the way it could. I didn't know if there were other ways to use it apart from sprinkling it over pictures, and I didn't know if it had the ability to make things magically good the way it could clearly make things magically bad. I didn't know who Ms. Charlemagne was or how the powder had gotten into her bag, and I didn't know how to find her and ask her about everything that had happened and if it were possible to fix it.

It all seemed so hopeless, but then as I dripped great drops of purple watercolor onto my picture, it suddenly occurred to me that I was going about solving my problem all wrong.

Instead of focusing on what I didn't know, I decided to turn the situation around and try to figure out what I *did* know.

So what *did* I know? I knew that Interference Powder interfered with things . . . *somehow*. I knew it didn't make any difference what the person using it intended, or even desired. I knew that *every* change it made seemed to be permanent—that is, it didn't wear off after a few hours or days. I knew that when it was asked to do something I thought was good, like change my test score to 100 or put Isobel on the stage at the

Brain-Busters Extravaganza or give me a nice singing voice, it somehow made those nice things not so nice. I knew that the more I tried to control it, the more it seemed to stick out its tongue at me.

I looked down at my pictures: Fred the dog, my mom looking serious, the purple flower. And then suddenly I knew what I had to do.

I looked around my desk for a sheet of paper that hadn't been blotted by purple watercolor paint, and set the paper down in front of me.

I can do this, I thought. I know how to do this now.

It was time to draw a picture of myself, a picture that answered the other question Dr. Ceres said every kid had to answer: *Who am I?* I thought. Then I smiled to myself. Dr. Ceres had been right. It sounded easy, but it was hard. I might not be able to write it down the way I had written down the things I wanted out of life, but I thought I might be able to draw it if I concentrated really hard.

Taking up my pencil, I drew my own body: long, skinny arms with fingers outstretched; and my legs in blue jeans, ending in ten little toes; my black sweater and my long brown hair in its usual undistinguished ponytail. Then I drew my face: straight nose, dimples, the big eyebrows my mom always told me I would grow into. My ears, unpierced no matter how much I'd begged until I turned sixteen, and my brown eyes opened wide. I worked hard on the picture, and not because I was trying to make myself seem prettier than

I actually was, or more confident, or smarter, but because I started to think of the picture as a real mirror, and I wanted to see who the person on the page was, since she was me.

And she *was* me! Oh, maybe I got the nose a little wrong, or I drew my eyes a bit too close together. But as the girl on the page became clearer and clearer, I looked into her eyes and I saw myself; and I thought: There she is. That's Nina Zabin from Wilton Street in the town of Princeton, the county of Mercer, the state of New Jersey, the country of the United States. Nina Zabin, for better or for worse: a girl who was stupid about some things and smart about others, a girl with a mother downstairs and a father she could hardly remember, a girl with one old friend and (just maybe) two new ones, a girl who might or might not ever get to sing on a stage in front of people, a girl whose future no one could tell, least of all me.

You might not be able to control Interference Powder, I thought, looking down at my own face. You might not be able to give it orders, or even requests. Not even polite suggestions! But maybe you could fig-ure out who you really are and what you really want and then step back and just believe in the magic, and in yourself, and in the idea that somehow everything will come out all right in the end. Maybe then Interference Powder would work right for a change.

I got up and went to my bedside table. I took out the envelope with the Interference Powder for what I knew would be the last time. Then I brought it over to the desk, sat down again, and slowly opened the envelope over my drawing. The little flakes sparkled as they fell through the air and bounced on the surface. It was so beautiful, I thought. Whatever else it was, it was just beautiful.

I sat very still for a long moment, trying not to think about what might happen now. I closed my eyes, hearing the sounds of the street, the faraway clatter of my mother's office door shutting as her patient left, the rustle of the squirrel that had escaped Fred's attentions and was running away through the trees. Everything was totally quiet, peaceful, and sweet.

Then, without even thinking about what I was going to do, I took a deep breath and blew hard at the page, and the Interference Powder went *whoosh* out the window, out into the clear autumn air that was already full of falling leaves. In an instant it was lost in the wind. Not a speck of it remained! The powder, which had come into my life so mysteriously, was gone forever, and I breathed a sigh of relief.

I got to my feet and shut the window. Suddenly, I was so tired, I could barely keep myself from falling over. I half stumbled to the bed, pulled the quilt over my head, and fell into a sleep so noiseless and heavy that not even a thunderclap could have wakened me.

chapter nineteen

"Nina! It's time for dinner!"

I sat up. The room was dark. I didn't know the time.

"Nina?"

"I'm coming," I shouted, and bolted out of bed and across the floor in my stockinged feet. I felt dizzy, still half-asleep, and it wasn't until my hand closed over the doorknob that I realized what had just happened.

I stopped, holding the doorknob for balance. In a whisper, I spoke into the dark room.

"I'm coming."

Yes! I thought. *Oh, absolutely, certainly, positively yes!*

It was a normal voice. A little bit rusty and a little bit breathy, but normal. It was my voice, back from Interference Powder Land.

"I'm coming, Mom!" I shouted joyfully. "I'll be right there!"

Seconds later I hurtled myself downstairs and into her arms. "I can talk!" I said, hugging her.

"So I hear." She laughed. "I'm very glad."

"Me, too!" I said, doing a little hop up and down. "Me, too!"

Then she told me to sit down because the lasagna was ready, and all of a sudden I felt hungrier than I'd ever been before. I thought I'd barely be able to wait till my dinner hit the table.

"Here," she said. "Toss up this salad."

I did. There were no red peppers this time. I was so happy, I felt like hugging my mom just for that.

"So, we never really talked about your appointment this morning," she said.

"I thought you're not supposed to talk about what goes on between a therapist and a patient," I teased, and she looked a little surprised.

"That's perfectly true." She was putting a big wedge of lasagna, steaming and dripping tomato sauce, on my plate. "You don't have to tell me a thing. I thought you might want to, that's all."

"No, it's okay." I took a huge bite: cheese, tomato, pasta, and onions all ran hotly together in my mouth. "He seems pretty nice," I said after I'd swallowed.

"Yes, he does, doesn't he?" my mother said evenly. "Is his daughter nice, too?"

"Very!" I nodded. "I should call her. Maybe she could come over this weekend."

My mother nodded. "Good. I'm glad you're making some other friends. Not that I don't love Isobel, but it's good to have a few friends, you know."

This took the wind out of my sails, a little bit. In fact, the thought of Isobel was the only thing that still hurt. After all, just because my voice was back didn't mean anything had changed between us.

"You know," Mom said, "it's one of the reasons I was so happy to see you do well on the social studies test. I've sometimes wondered if you might be holding yourself back in school."

"Holding myself back?" I said, looking at her.

"Sure," she said, spearing a tomato. "Because of Isobel. Because you didn't want to compete with her by doing well with your schoolwork. You know, it's something your dad used to say about you: 'Those girls have just decided that Isobel's the smart one and Nina's the artistic one.'"

"My dad said that?" I asked in surprise. Isobel and I had only been four years old when my dad died.

My mom was nodding. "He was very insightful that way," she said with a faraway kind of look. "But we were talking about you." She smiled at me.

"This is more interesting," I said quickly. "What else did my dad say?"

"Oh." Mom sighed. "Let's see. He said he would never want to be married to someone who agreed with him about everything, because that wouldn't be very interesting. He said he could never love a woman who played golf. He said that when he was a little boy, he had a playmate who died in an accident, and every day after that he tried to set aside a few minutes to find some wonderful thing in the world and be happy about it." She stopped. She looked at me. "He said the worst thing about getting sick and knowing he was probably not going to live very much longer was how he would miss watching you grow up. He loved you so much."

I looked down at my hands. "I wish I remembered him."

"Me too. But it isn't your fault that you can't. You were very young." She smiled.

My mom got up and filled her water glass at the sink. Then, without even thinking about it, I said, "Why don't you ever go out on dates? You could, you know. I mean, I wouldn't mind."

She sat down again and looked at me intently. "It's funny that you should say that," she said. "Because I've actually been thinking of going on a date."

"Really?"

"Well, yes. I met someone kind of interesting. He might ask me out." She smiled at me. "Or then again, I might ask him."

"Well!" I said. I was, of course, dying to ask who this person was.

But then, quite suddenly, I knew who it was. Even without asking I knew. It was Dr. Serious! (I mean, Dr. Ceres. I'd never get used to his real name.) I just knew it was him.

She sat back in her chair. "And I have something to tell you, Nina."

What now? I thought.

"I've arranged for you to take a singing lesson."

I stared at her in shock. Was it possible? What on earth had gotten into her?

"I think you're entitled to know the essence of my conversation with Dr. Ceres this morning. In fact, he had some very interesting insights into what brought on your difficulty with speech."

"Oh yes?" I said carefully.

"Yes. He thought you had chosen a very creative way to let me know how important singing was to you. So I am willing to let you try this. I spoke with a singing teacher this afternoon, and she's agreed to meet with you tomorrow. She wants to hear you sing and see if the two of you would be able to work together. Sound good?"

"Sounds great!" I yelped. "Oh, Mom, you've made me really happy."

"Well, good." She got up to put her plate in the sink. "I try never to miss an opportunity to make the people I love happy."

After dinner she went upstairs to call Aunt Sally and find out whether she had found her passion, and I went back to my room.

I was far too keyed up to do anything, so I ended up sitting cross-legged on my bed, thinking, Singing lessons! I'm starting singing lessons tomorrow!

I remembered what Mom had said about the teacher wanting to hear me sing, and to my surprise, I wasn't the slightest bit nervous about that. After all, one thing I had gotten out of the Brain-Busters Extravaganza had been some experience singing in front of a large audience, so how hard could it be to sing for only one person after that?

I wondered how my mom had managed to find me a singing teacher so quickly, within hours of talking it over with Dr. Ceres! And I wondered what kind of person she would be. An old, distinguished lady with a European accent? A young music student from the choir college in town? A mean, strict instructor who would *tsk, tsk* if I didn't hit the right notes?

Would I like her?

Would she like me?

When my mom finally got off the phone with Aunt Sally, I went to call Isobel and tell her the great news, but then I stopped myself. I still wasn't sure what to do about Isobel, but I hoped—I really hoped—that I would hear from her soon. I missed her more than ever.

It was late, and I had an important appointment the next day. I changed into a nightgown, but I left my socks on my feet because it was cold; and then I got under the covers. Before I fell asleep, I sang every song I could remember into the dark room.

chapter twenty

When I woke up the next day, I threw on my clothes and went rushing into my mom's bedroom, ready to tear across town to my lesson.

"I'm ready!" I shouted, jumping on her bed.

"Ready for what?" My mother groaned. "Oh . . ." She turned over. "It isn't till noon."

"Noon!" I said, annoyed. How was I supposed to wait till then?

"I gotta sleep," she said. "I was up late on the phone."

"No you weren't!" I protested. "I heard you hang up. You talked to Aunt Sally for ages, but it wasn't that late."

There was a pause. "Different call," she said finally. "All right?"

I looked at her. She didn't open her eyes. But she did smile.

"All right," I said. I went to the door of her bedroom. "So. Are we going out on a date?"

She flopped over on her back and peered at me. "*We're* not. But as it happens, *I* am."

Well!

I let her go back to sleep and went downstairs to get a glass of orange juice. As I poured it, I heard the slap of a footstep on our porch and then a little knock at the door.

I knew that knock.

I flew to the door and let in Isobel. As if nothing had ever happened, I grinned at her and said, "Is! I've got a singing lesson today!"

Her mouth dropped open. "Oh, wow! How'd you talk your mom into it?"

"I didn't." I grabbed her wrist and pulled her into the kitchen. "She just . . . I don't know why she changed her mind," I lied, "but she did. And my first lesson is in four hours!"

It was nice to see how happy she was. She's still my friend! I thought happily.

Then I paused. Had she stopped *not* being my friend? Or had Interference Powder switched things around so she had *never* not been my friend? I peered at her suspiciously.

Isobel looked down at the table. "I don't blame you for looking at me like that," she said quietly. "I've been pretty mean to you. I'm here to say I'm sorry."

So she was *back* to being my friend!

"Sorry?" I said.

"Yeah. You do better than me by one point on one stupid test and I act like you're a criminal or some-thing."

"It's all right." I shrugged.

"No. It isn't. I should have congratulated you."

I sighed. "Let's just forget about it, okay? Besides, it was no fun at all being a Brain-Buster, let me tell you."

"No." She giggled. "I could tell you were miserable. In fact, I was a little worried about you."

"A little!" I rolled my eyes.

"When you sang like that. Of course, you sounded great, but it was kind of . . ."

"Unexpected? I was just really nervous, that's all."

"And then that pipe breaking!"

"Saved by the pipe!" I laughed. I went to the refrigerator, poured her a glass of orange juice, and led her out to our front porch. We didn't have any chairs on our porch, so we sat on the top step.

"I've been feeling so rotten," she confided, sipping her juice. "My mom asked me last night why you hadn't been over, and I just started crying and told her everything about that ridiculous test. She said I'd feel a lot better when I apologized." Isobel looked at me shyly. "She was right, of course."

"They usually are," I agreed. "Moms are so annoying that way."

We both grinned. Then I remembered something.

"What about Drea Wells? The two of you were practically glued together."

"Oh, please!" Is put up her hands. "Don't speak the name Drea Wells out loud. She's always on the phone: 'Isobel! Come play a video game in my basement!'

'Isobel! Come over and let's paint our fingernails!'"

"Well, maybe you shouldn't have encouraged her!" I teased.

"I didn't. She just . . ." Isobel gave me an embarrassed look. "She just saw we weren't getting along, and she moved in. I'm trying to be polite, but I don't really want to hang out with her." I looked down the street. Fred the dog was taking his owner for a walk on a leash.

"I hung out with Ella Ceres. And Theo Matza," I told Isobel. "We studied together. They're both so nice."

There was an unspoken part of this sentence. It was: *We should maybe give them a call sometime.*

Isobel heard this unspoken part and considered it. Then she nodded. "Yeah. They do seem nice. So." She turned to me. "Want to come over for dinner tonight?"

I raised an eyebrow at her. "Depends," I said.

"Depends on what?" She frowned, looking a little worried.

"On what your mom is cooking. What else?"

chapter
twenty-one

The teacher was called Ms. Mayne, and I walked down Pine Street a few hours later with my stomach full of fluttering butterflies. I was holding a piece of paper with her address, and it got clammier and clammier in my hand as I neared the end of the street.

Pine Street was in a part of town called the Tree Street neighborhood, where all of the streets had names like Linden and Maple. Pine was narrow and full of old, slightly tippy houses, and Ms. Mayne's turned out to be one of the oldest and tippiest of all. It was gray and set back a bit from the street, with lots of purple mums planted out front. The curtains were drawn, and my heart pounded as I climbed up the steps to the front door.

I lifted an old brass knocker and let it fall: *clank.*

At first there was nothing but silence.

Then, from inside, a shuffle.

"Just a minute!" The voice was high and light. A happy voice. I didn't think it belonged to an old, distinguished European lady. I didn't think it belonged to a mean instructor who was likely to say *"Tsk! Tsk!,"* either.

The door swung open.

I don't mind telling you, I nearly fell over, right there on the top step.

"Hey!" said the very surprising person who stood there. "Whoa! Steady! Are you all right?"

"I've been looking everywhere for you!" I managed to sputter. I grabbed at the handrail.

"Well, you found me. Come on inside. You must be Serena Zabin's daughter."

"And you're Charlemagne!" I nearly shouted.

She looked at me oddly. The little bells braided into her hair caught the light. "Wait a minute. Have we met before?"

"At my school!" I shouted. I was itching to ask her about a hundred questions, all at the same time. "You came to my school! You taught my art class!"

"Oh. Yes!" She smiled, motioning me to follow her into the living room. It was small, with some comfortable-looking chairs and a braided rug. "I substitute teach. They called me that morning."

"I looked for you!" I said, walking behind her. "I looked in the phone book. I looked up Charlemagnes all over the country!"

This made her laugh, and she threw back her head to do it. "Oh, you poor thing! Charlemagne! Like the French king, right?"

Confused and exasperated, I nodded.

"Well, it isn't that. It's Charla. C-H-A-R-L-A. Because my father was named Charles. Now, if I'd been a boy, I would have been Charles, too; but Charla was the best they could do for a girl. And Mayne is our last name. Oh, don't worry." She smiled merrily. "You're hardly the first one. I don't think my parents realized when they named me Charla that it wasn't the best choice to go with our last name. One of my aunts put it together pretty quickly—Charlemagne!—but by then it was too late. All the forms were filled out. So every now and then somebody comes up to me with this big joke. I'm used to it, though." She shook her head so quickly, the bells braided into her hair gave a tinkle.

"I went to the school and asked about you. I said I wanted to take art lessons. Remember? You told me that you give art lessons at home!"

"Oh." she smiled. "I might have told you I give lessons in my home, but I'm quite certain I never said I give *art* lessons. I give *singing* lessons. But I don't think I ever heard from you."

"They wouldn't give me your address, but they said they'd forward my letter to you. Maybe they forgot," I told her.

"Maybe," Charla Mayne said thoughtfully. "Let's see." She turned and walked over to a table by the door. On the table was a great stack of mail, tipping dangerously. Charla Mayne did not strike me as the most organized of individuals, but I guess that went along with being an artist. She started flipping through the stack, tossing circulars and catalogs onto thefloor. "Yes, look!" she said, holding up a long, white envelope. "This looks promising." She opened up the flap and extracted a smaller, blue envelope I recognized as my own. She opened that, too, and read aloud. "'Dear Ms. Charlemagne, would you please tell me how I can reach you? I need to ask you about something. It's very urgent.'"

She looked thoughtfully down at the letter for a moment. Then she turned and walked into her kitchen and started filling her kettle with water. "Let's have some tea," she said. "I mean chamomile tea, of course. If you're going to sing, you're going to have to start taking care of your throat."

"Okay," I said.

She bustled around the kitchen, fixing our tea, and set a steaming mug before me as we sat down at the table. "And now, Serena Zabin's daughter, whom I met in art class at Riverside School and who wants to take singing lessons, may I be so bold as to ask why you had to talk to me so urgently?"

Because, I told her as calmly as I could, of Interference Powder.

She merely looked at me. "What?"

"Interference Powder! From the bag you brought to my art class!"

Still, she frowned. "The bag?"

"The art bag! Remember how you told me to find some colors in your bag? Well, I found something else. It turned my whole life upside down. It's . . ." I leaned forward, and I said the word. I said: "Magic."

Charla Mayne looked at me as if I were utterly nuts.

So I told her everything. About how my 62 became 100, about how I became a Brain-Buster, about how I drew Isobel, about the tear on the picture and the burst water pipe, about my drawing of myself singing and how I couldn't speak after that, only sing. I told her about the last picture I drew and how my voice came back and Isobel came to my house and my mother said I could have singing lessons, and how I blew away every last speck of Interference Powder.

"But I can prove it!" I told her. "Let's look in the bag. I put the little jar of powder back in there. You can see for yourself."

She seemed far from convinced, but she excused herself and went upstairs. I heard doors open and cupboards shut as she hunted; and then she returned, stepping heavily down the carpeted stairs, carrying the bag itself. She placed it on the table between us, and we both looked at it in silence for a minute. All of a sudden I didn't want to see that little glass vial again. I didn't want to be tempted by it, and I didn't want anyone else to get into the kind of trouble I'd just gotten myself out of.

Charla Mayne opened the leather bag. The smell of old paints drifted out, and we could hear the tinkle of glass. She reached in and slowly lifted out the jars of old, crusted colors; the brushes; an old rag so stiff, it was almost like a piece of wood. Then, just when it seemed that my vial— the vial that had caused so much uproar in my life—must have vanished, she brought it out, pinched between her thumb and forefinger. I stared at it. There they were, those colorless flakes that had come alive as bright colors when I shook them and done so much else when I let them fall over my drawings. And there was the little label that read in tiny writing, Interference Powder.

"Well, my word," Charla Mayne said softly. "What do

you know? I actually remember this!"

I kept quiet, hoping she would say more.

"I had an art teacher in college. Quite a strange old lady. She had lived in Paris in the 1920s and even knew Pablo Picasso!"

"Really?" I said, very impressed. Isobel's mom had written a whole book about Pablo Picasso.

"I thought I wanted to be a painter then, but something happened that made me change my mind. Afterward I decided to concentrate on my voice."

This was getting interesting. "What happened?" I said, leaning forward.

"Oh, it was a crazy thing. One day I went to the studio, and my teacher gave me this vial. She said to mix a bit of the powder in with my paints. I didn't know why, but I was a little afraid of her so I did what she told me."

"Afraid of her?" I frowned.

"Oh," Charla Mayne laughed, and the bells in her hair tinkled. "She was terribly fierce. She used to say, 'Miss Mayne! You must have passion to be a painter! You must *need* to be a painter! Otherwise, you must not paint!' I did need to be a painter, or I thought I did; but that day . . . Well, the strangest thing happened. We were all supposed to paint a bowl of fruit that our teacher set up in front of the room. I remember the fruit! There were three pomegranates and an avocado! But when I set out to paint them, I ended up painting a piano. And it was the oddest thing, because I kept trying. Over and over again I started out with a clean canvas and tried to paint those pomegranates and that avocado, and it just kept coming out a piano. Everyone in the class was laughing at me, but I couldn't stop myself. Doesn't that sound strange?"

Not at all, I was thinking. Not when there was Interference Powder involved.

"And afterward this woman, my teacher, took me out for tea and asked me why I thought I wanted to be a painter; and instead I ended up telling her how much I wanted to sing! It was such a funny thing, because until that moment I hadn't figured that out for myself."

"And that's how you became a singer," I said.

"Yes. Well, that's when I knew. Of course, I still enjoy painting, but singing became my life."

Charla Mayne held up the little vial. "I must have forgotten to give this back," she said, frowning a little.

She gave it a little shake, and once again the colorless flakes resting on the bottom of the vial began to jump into color: reds and greens. For a moment I forgot what a nightmare those flakes had caused and was lost in their fleeting beauty. But I totally snapped out of it when I saw that Charla was beginning to unscrew the cap.

"Now," she said amiably, "how did you say it worked?"

"No, don't!" I shouted. "Honest, you don't want to. I told you, it *interferes*. You want to leave it alone. You really do."

She looked at me in surprise. It was obvious that she didn't believe the rest of my story, but she put the vial back in the bag and closed it with a satisfying click. Then she set the bag on the kitchen floor and looked at me thoughtfully. "You know," she said finally, "I don't have many students now. And I almost never take on a new one. But I made an exception in your case."

"You did?" I asked, blushing. "But why? You've never heard me sing, have you?" A horrible thought occurred to me. What if she had been there the day of the Brain-Busters Extravaganza? What if she had been substitute teaching again and had joined the throng in the auditorium to witness my most humiliating moment?

She shook her head, and the beads tinkled merrily. "No. But I owe your mother a good deal."

I stared at her. "My mother?"

"Absolutely. I went to see her last year because I hadn't been able to sing in front of an audience for a very long time. I had developed such stage fright, it was torture to use my voice. I was terribly unhappy about it, because not only had I always loved to perform, but it was my livelihood, you see. So I began seeing your mother." She looked at me squarely. "Your mother is a wonderful therapist. Did you know that?"

Did I know that? I suppose I had always known that, though she never told me much about her patients. I was only just realizing that Charla was the patient Mom had described to me, the one who had not been able to use her gift and whom my mother had helped by using the best parts of herself.

"So now we come to you," said Charla. "And to your voice." She turned to face me. "Here's how it works, Nina. You may have a voice that's perfectly nice, but which you're unable to manipulate. We call this an untrainable voice. You may have a voice that doesn't sound so nice right now, but it can be worked with. This is a trainable voice. How you sound at this moment means less than what I can hear in your voice. Do you see?"

I nodded.

"But many people have voices that are trainable. In itself that's not enough to justify my time, or frankly yours. I'm looking for something extra. A little spark. Something that isn't connected to how much you *want* to use your voice."

Now I was a little confused. "What kind of spark?"

"Well." She sighed a little. "I suppose it's a bit like your magic powder. You bring something to the project: your desire to learn to sing and your trainable voice. But the something extra is the magic. It takes those things and it, well . . . I suppose you could say it *interferes* with them. It's the difference between hearing a hundred people sing a song in a pleasant voice that's in tune and then hearing the hundred-and-first person sing the same song and bring tears to your eyes or make you want to leap to your feet and applaud."

She paused to let what she had said sink in. By this point I was feeling very small, indeed.

"And now, Nina, I think I am ready to hear you sing something. Just by yourself. No need to go upstairs to the piano yet. What would you like to sing?"

I felt a shiver of nerves. Every song I had *ever* learned seemed to fly from my brain.

But then, suddenly, I had a brilliant idea. "What about . . . 'Yankee Doodle Dandy'?" I grinned. And then I opened my mouth and sang.

chapter
twenty-two

As I walked down Wilton Street late that afternoon, I saw a brown United Parcel Service truck pull out of our driveway. It had deposited an enormous package on our front porch, and my mother was staring at it with her hands on her hips. By the time I reached our mailbox, she was slicing away at the tape with a kitchen knife.

"What's that?" I asked, coming up the porch steps.

"Oh, Nina!" My mother turned. "That must have been the longest singing lesson on record! Was it all right?"

"You could say that." I smiled.

"And did you sing?"

"Yes. She says I have a trainable voice. And a spark. I think that's good."

My mother nodded. "Yes, I would say it was."

"What's in the package?" I asked, stepping around it.

"Well, this"—my mother went back to cutting the tape—"this, my dear Nina, unless I'm much mistaken, is your aunt Sally's passion. She told me last night on the phone that she had sent it. It arrived quickly!"

She cut the last bit of tape and pulled down one side of

the cardboard. Inside stood an enormous chair made of wood and painted white, with great, fat, green flowers stenciled all over it. It was shaped like a cushy soft armchair, but of course there were no cushions anywhere on it, just slats of wood. Even so, it made you want to leap into it and put up your feet, balance your glass of iced tea on one of the big armrests and your book on the other, and just dream away the day.

"It's fantastic!" I said. "I love it! I can't believe she made it!"

"You won't believe this, either," my mother said, removing a little note that had been taped to the backrest. It's called the 'Nina Chair.' She named it after you."

"No kidding!" I grinned. I hadn't known chairs had names. And what a great chair to have my name!

"So that's it for being a real estate lawyer," said my mom. "This is what she loves, and she's obviously got a real feeling for it. I don't think I realized when she told me she'd been making chairs, just how beautiful they were." She stood, looking thoughtfully at it. "You know, I'd like another one. It'd be nice to have two, wouldn't it? One for each of us. I'll commission her to make us another, all right?"

"'Nina Chair, the Sequel.'" I laughed. "Great idea."

"Oh, that reminds me." I looked at her. She was trying not to smile. "You had a call while you were out. A Mr. Theodore Matza."

"Hmm," I said.

"Seems he would like to take you to the movies. Well,

what he actually said was, 'I'm calling to ask Nina if it would be okay if I asked her to go to the movies.'" She laughed. "He's adorable."

"Yeah, yeah," I said, looking off down the street. "I guess I should call him back."

"Guess you should," said my mom.

I went inside. Something was nagging at me, some little itch at the back of my thoughts. It had begun with the arrival of the chair and grown stronger with the news about Theo's phone call. There was something familiar about all this, something I couldn't put my finger on.

I started up the stairs.

Not that I had anything to worry about. Things were going great! Isobel was my friend again, I'd just had my first singing lesson, my mom had a date, and my aunt Sally had found her passion. And even Theo had asked me to go to the movies. It was all . . .

It was all exactly as I had wished when I wrote out that list for Dr. Ceres.

I stopped right there on the stairs.

I was trying to remember exactly what I had done with that piece of stationery from Dr. Ceres's office.

I raced into my room and started looking around for it.

It wasn't shoved into the pocket of my jeans. It wasn't on the floor. It wasn't in my bedside table drawer. It wasn't in the wastebasket.

I wouldn't have left it in Dr. Ceres's office! No way would I have risked his finding and reading it. I wouldn't have lost it. . . . How could I lose something so important and so private?

That's when my eye fell on the plain white sheets that were all over my desk, the ones I had used the day before when I had painted Fred and my mom and the purple flower, and then drawn my final picture and sprinkled it with Interference Powder. The sheets lay scattered about, surrounding and partially covering the drawing itself. The glops of purple watercolor I'd used had dried up by now or been soaked into some of the white pages, making the whole thing look pretty messy. Very carefully, I began to turn over the sheets, one by one, searching for the lost piece of stationery, putting each piece of paper aside as I saw it wasn't the one I was looking for. It wasn't there. It wasn't there, and it wasn't there.

At last the table was bare except for the picture itself, and I stood for a long moment looking down at the girl I had drawn, the girl who actually was me. I think I knew, looking down at that picture, what was going to happen. I think maybe I had known ever since my mom had told me about Theo calling to ask me to go to the movies.

I turned my picture over and sure enough, there it was: the stationery of Dr. Brian Ceres covered with the list of things I wanted. I read through that list again.
I WANT ISOBEL TO BE MY FRIEND AGAIN. I WANT MY MOM TO BE HAPPY. I DON'T WANT HER TO BE LONELY. I WANT MY AUNT SALLY TO FIND HER PASSION. I WANT ELLA TO BE MY FRIEND. I WANT THEO TO ASK ME TO GO TO THE MOVIES. I WANT

TO KNOW THE PERSON I REALLY AM, DEEP DOWN, SO I CAN BE TRUE TO THAT PERSON AND STOP WORRYING ABOUT THE THINGS I'M PROBABLY NEVER GOING TO BE VERY GOOD AT. I WOULD REALLY, REALLY, REALLY LIKE TO TAKE SINGING LESSONS.

Of all the pieces of paper on my desk, I had somehow come to draw my picture on the back of that one, and for once Interference Powder hadn't backfired. It had given me everything I had asked for, as if I had made out some kind of Christmas list! Was it because, as Dr. Ceres said, I was finally asking myself who Nina was and what Nina wanted and what Nina could offer the world? I had no idea, and I knew better than to try and figure it out. Interference Powder was magic, after all, and you just can't figure out magic.

I looked again at my drawing.

A great blot of dried purple watercolor paint had soaked through the pictures of Mom, Fred, and the pink-and-purple flower to my feet in the drawing of myself. Looking at those purple feet, I started to get a funny feeling.

I sat down and took off my running shoes. Then I pulled down those socks that hadn't been off my feet since yesterday. What do you think I saw?

Oh, that's right—I've already told you, way back at the beginning of my story! So now you know about my purple toenails and how they got that way. But to tell you the truth, I don't mind that much. I've always liked purple, and when you think about it, it's a small price to pay for the adventure I've had and for all of the great stuff that's happened.

But let me tell you one last thing. If you ever come across these strange little flakes that wiggle their way into your life and give you some things you really wanted and some things you didn't *know* you really wanted but leave you with a case of permanent toenail polish, then my best advice is to keep your socks on and say no more about it.